ATLANTA
DEATHWATCH

The Hardman Series

ATLANTA DEATHWATCH

RALPH DENNIS

Introduction "Ralph Dennis & Hardman"
Copyright © 2018 by Joe R. Lansdale. All Rights Reserved.

Cover Photograph of the Ford Maverick by Accord14, licensed under CC
BY-SA 4.0, https://commons.wikimedia.org/w/index.php?curid=52131087

ISBN: 1-7320656-6-7
ISBN-13: 978-1-732-06566-6

Published by Brash Books, LLC
12120 State Line #253,
Leawood, Kansas 66209
www.brash-books.com

INTRODUCTION

Ralph Dennis and Hardman
By Joe R. Lansdale

Once upon the time there were a lot of original paperbacks, and like the pulps before them, they covered a lot of ground. Western, adventure, romance, mystery, science fiction, fantasy, and crime, for example.

There were also subsets of certain genres. One of those was the sexy, men's action-adventure novel with a dab of crime and mystery.

These books had suggestive titles, or indicators that not only were they action packed with blood and sweat, fists and bullets, but that there would be hot, wet sex. They were straight up from the male reader's perspective, the perspective of the nineteen seventies and early eighties.

There were entire lines of adult westerns for example. They sold well at the time. Quite well. These Westerns sold so well, that for a brief period it seemed as if it might go on forever. They made up the largest number of Westerns on the stands rivaled only by Louis L'Amour, and a few reprints from Max Brand and Zane Grey.

An agent once told me I was wasting my time writing other things, and I could be part of this big stable he had writing adult Westerns. Although I had nothing against sexy Westerns, which may in fact have been pioneered as a true branch of the Western genre by a very good writer named Brian Garfield and his novel *Sliphammer*, but I didn't want to spend a career writing them. Not the sort I had read, anyway.

Still, a small part of me, the part that was struggling to pay bills, thought maybe I could write something of that nature that might be good enough to put a pen name on. Many of my friends and peers were doing it, and some actually did it quite well, but if ever there was a formulaic brand of writing, that was it.

I was a big fan of Westerns in general, however, so I thought I might could satisfy that itch, while managing to satisfy the publisher's itch, not to mention that of the Adult Western reader, primarily males.

I picked up a number of the so called adult Westerns, read them, and even landed a job as a ghost for one series, but the publisher and the writer had a falling out, so my work was never published, though I got paid.

Actually, for me, that was the best-case scenario. Once I started on the series I knew I was in for trouble. It wasn't any fun for me, and that is the main reason I write. I woke up every morning feeling ill because I was trying to write that stuff. It was like trying to wear a tux to a tractor pull.

I thought, maybe there's something I would like more in the action-adventure line, crime, that sort of thing. I had read *The Executioner*, and had even written three in the *M.I.A. Hunter* series, and frankly, next to nailing my head to a burning building, I would rather have been doing anything else. But a look at our bank account made me more pliable.

But that was later. At the time I was looking at this sort of genre, trying to understand if there was anything in it I could truly like, I picked up a book by Ralph Dennis, *The Charleston Knife is Back in Town*, bearing the overall title of *Hardman*. The books were billed by the publisher as "a great new private eye for the shockproof seventies."

The title was suggestive in a non-subtle way, and I remember sighing, and cracking it open and hoping I could at least make it a third of the way through.

And then, it had me. It gripped me and carried me through, and one thing was immediately obvious. It wasn't a sex and shoot novel. It's not that those were not components, but not in the way of the other manufactured series, where sometimes the sex scenes were actually lifted from another one in the series and placed in the new one, in the perfunctory manner you might replace a typewriter ribbon.

I was working on a typewriter in those days, and so was everyone else. If that reference throws you, look it up. You'll find it somewhere between etched stone tablets and modern PCs.

Dennis wrote with assurance, and he built characterization through spot on first person narration. His prose was muscular, swift, and highly readable. There was an echo behind it.

Jim Hardman wasn't a sexy private eye with six-pack abs and face like Adonis. He was a pudgy, okay looking guy, and as a reader, you knew who Hardman was and how he saw things, including himself, in only a few pages.

You learned about him through dialogue and action. Dennis was good at both techniques. His action was swift and realistic, and you never felt as if something had been mailed in.

Hardman wasn't always likable, or good company. And he knew that about himself. He was a guy just trying to make it from day to day in a sweltering city. He had a friend named Hump, though Hardman was reluctant to describe him as such. In his view he and Hump were associates. He sometimes hired Hump to help him with cases where two men, and a bit of muscle, were needed.

That said, Hump was obviously important to Hardman, and as the series proceeded, he was more so. The books developed their world, that hot, sticky, Atlanta landscape, and it was also obvious that Dennis knew Atlanta well, or was at least able to give you the impression he did.

His relationship with Marcy, his girlfriend, had a convenient feel, more than that of a loving relationship, and it was off again and on again; it felt real, and the thing that struck me about the books was that there was real human fabric to them. There was action, of course, but like Chandler and Hammett before him, Dennis was trying to do something different with what was thought of as throw away literature.

I'm not suggesting Dennis was in the league of those writers, but he was certainly head and shoulders above the mass of paperbacks being put out fast and dirty. When I read Dennis's Hardman novels, the characters, the background, stayed with me. The stories were peripheral in a way. Like so many of the best modern crime stories, they were about character.

Due to the publishing vehicle and the purpose of the series, at least from the publisher's view point, the books sometimes showed a hastiness that undercut the best of the work, but, damn, I loved them. I snatched them up and devoured them.

I thought I might like to do something like that, but didn't, and a few years later I wrote those *M.I.A. Hunters*, which I actually loathed, and knew all my visitations with that branch of the genre I loved, crime and suspense, had ended, and not well, at least for me, though the three books were later collected and published in a hardback edition from Subterranean Press by me and its creator, Stephen Mertz.

A few years after that journey into the valley of death, quite a few, actually, I had a contract with Bantam, and I was trying to come up with a crime novel, and I wrote about this guy named Hap standing out in a field in East Texas, and with him, out of nowhere, was a gay, black guy named Leonard.

The idea of a black and white team in the depths of East Texas would be something I could write about, and it was a way for me to touch on social issues without having to make a parade of it. I thought, yeah, that'll work for me, and though my characters are quite different than Hardman, they share many similarities as well. The black and white team and Southern background (East Texas is more South than Southwestern), was certainly inspired by the Hardman novels. I think because it rang a bell with me, the clapper of that bell slapped up against my own personal experience, though mine was more rural than urban.

Even more than other writer heroes of mine, Chandler and Chester Himes for example, Hardman spoke directly to me. Chandler's language and wise cracks fit the people I grew up with, and Himes wrote about the black experience, something that was vital to the South, though often given a sideways consideration and the back of culture's hand. But Hardman had that white blue collar feel, even if he was in the city and was already an established, if unlicensed, private investigator and thug for hire. I blended all those writers, and many more, to make Hap and Leonard, John D. McDonald, certainly, but if I had a spirit guide with the Hap and Leonard books, it was Ralph Dennis.

So now we have the Hardman books coming back into print.

I am so excited about this neglected series being brought back, put in front of readers again. It meant a lot to me back then, and it still means a lot. You can beef about the deficiency of political correctness, but twenty years from now they'll be beefing about our lack of political correctness on some subject or another that we now think we are hip to. And too much political correctness is the enemy of truth, and certainly there are times when fiction is not about pretty manners but should ring the true bells of social conditions and expression. Erasing what is really going on, even in popular fiction, doesn't do anyone any favors. Righteous political correctness has its place, but political correct police do not.

I know very little about Ralph Dennis. I know this. He wrote other books outside the Hardman series. I don't think he had the career he deserved. The Hardman books were a product of their time, but they managed to be about their time, not of it. They stand head and shoulders above so much of the paperback fodder that was designed for men to hold the book in one hand, and something else in the other. And I don't mean a can of beer.

But one thing is for sure, these books are still entertaining, and they are a fine time capsule that addresses the nature and attitudes of the time in which they were written. They do that with clean, swift prose, sharp characterization, and an air of disappointment in humanity that seems more and more well-earned.

I'm certainly glad I picked that Hardman novel up those long years ago. They were just what I needed. An approach that imbedded in my brain like a knitting needle, mixed with a variety of other influences, and helped me find my own voice. An authentic Southern voice. A voice that wasn't that of New York or Los Angeles or Chicago, but a voice of the South.

Thanks Ralph Dennis for helping me recognize that my background was as good a fodder for popular fiction as any, and that popular fiction could attempt to rise above the common crime novel. I don't know that I managed that, but Ralph Dennis was one of those writers that made me try.

Dennis may not have made literature of Hardman, but he damn sure touched on it more than a time or two, and I wish you the joy I got from first reading these novels, so many long, years ago.

Read on.

PUBLISHER'S NOTE

This book was originally published in 1974 and reflects the cultural and sexual attitudes, language, and politics of the period.

CHAPTER ONE

There was a blizzard, or what looked like one, up in New York City. In the TV news footage the snow drifts looked about hip high. And there was a sleet storm over Maryland and Virginia. But here in Atlanta the sun was out all day and the temperature was in the low 60's. It began to drop around dusk, and the wind was up. Now it was in the upper 40's and holding, and that was fine for me. I didn't want it any lower. I'd had enough of sitting around in parked cars in freezing weather, waiting for my feet to turn into ice cubes. I guess that's a sign I'm getting old, but I don't like to think so.

It was a simple tail, a follow-around for the evening and report-back in the morning—that kind of thing. Like most of that kind of work, it was a goddamn bore. Most of the evening I was in my '65 Ford, parked at a slight angle across the street from the Dew Drop In Cafe. Every half-hour or so, I'd leave the car and cross the street. I'd pass the cafe and look in. Each time, so far, she'd been there. Emily Campbell, 19, blonde and pretty, hunched over the bar sipping a glass of beer. There were eight or ten other drinkers in the place and they were all black. What interested me was that there were exactly two empty bar stools on each side of her. None of the studs seemed to be trying to make time.

The last pass by the cafe, a big stud with an Afro turned slowly on his stool and stared at me past the neon sputter of the cafe sign. That stare curdled my blood a bit, and I thought about calling Hump and having him drop into the cafe and see what he could find out from the inside. Hump's black, and that's a great disguise in the part of town I was operating in this Friday night, the 10th of December.

I decided against calling Hump. The fee for the tail was too low, and it wouldn't do to split two ways. On the way back to the car my blood started flowing again and the hard ridge of muscle high in my back relaxed. It was just routine. Nothing to worry about.

The phone call earlier in the day shouldn't have surprised me. The state legislature was in special session, and I usually got some work out of the members' back-alley merry-making. Mainly nasty little jobs. Things I'd straighten out, so the folks back home wouldn't hear about them. The first favor I'd done was for old Hugh Muffin, a long-time state senator from the south-eastern part of the state. It involved some pictures of Hugh being blown by a 16-year-old hippie chick. The pictures, according to the chick and her boyfriend, were worth ten thousand dollars. Hump had talked to the boyfriend in the bathroom of the little apartment in the 10th Street area, and I'd reasoned with the girl in the bedroom. In the end, we had the prints and the negatives and they had a few new bruises.

After that, there were other jobs. A few bucks here and a few bucks there. Some of them came through Hugh and others by way of the legislative grapevine. In this new job there'd been no mention of Hugh, though I knew that he and my new client, Arch Campbell, were drinking friends. Maybe Hugh had suggested me. Maybe not. Anyway, the job seemed simple enough. Arch Campbell had a daughter at Tech. Apple of his eye and only child and all that. Now, according to him, it looked like she was headed for hell in a handbasket. After a fine freshman year, dean's list, her grades were down, and she'd decided against going into her mother's sorority. She wouldn't return her mother's calls. Twice her mother had driven out to Tech to see her, and both times she'd been out. My job was to tail her around for a day or two and find out what was distracting her. That was fifty dollars a day, flat fee.

I started the job in the late afternoon. I drove out to Tech and found her dormitory without any trouble. Then I cruised around the parking lot until I spotted her green Toyota with the tag numbers the old man had given me. I parked in a space two rows behind her, and walked around until I found a pay phone. From the noise in Arch Campbell's room at the Regency, it sounded like they were having a hell of a party. He had to shush them down before we could talk.

"Call your daughter," I told him, "and say you're coming right over to see her."

"I don't understand..."

"Say you'll be there in ten minutes."

"If you say so, I will, but..."

I said, "Do it right now," and hung up.

I got back to my car and waited. Sure enough, about six or seven minutes later, a girl came running out the side entrance of the dorm. She was fumbling her arms into a sweater and looking around as if she expected the devil himself to appear. She got into the green Toyota and burned rubber leaving the parking lot. A block or so later, the panic seemed to drain out of her and she eased down to fit into the traffic. I fell into place two cars back and relaxed. She was a driving-manual driver, and it wasn't hard to keep her in sight.

When she reached West Peachtree and North, she turned and headed downtown. She went through the main part of Peachtree and reached Whitehall. I was right behind her then. When she took an abrupt right into a service station, got out, and went to a phone booth. From where I was, she seemed upset. She had slammed the receiver down hard on the final call. Right after that, she'd driven to the Dew Drop In Cafe. That was almost four hours ago, and she was still there. If she was waiting for someone, as I guessed, then that someone was a few hours late.

It was time to check on her again. I didn't relish that much, not after the big black with the Afro had taken that hard look at me. But if she took a quick run out the back door, I'd have to start over again the next day, and I didn't want that, either. I was sitting there, debating with myself, when a set of headlights struck the back window and lit me up. A car eased to the curb behind me. I leaned down and got the slapjack from under the seat. I placed it on the seat beside me and, as the headlights went out, I turned and saw two blacks get out of the car. One was on the walk side and the other on the street side. They were arguing and raising a lot of good-natured hell, like they'd already had a few to drink. The one on the walk said he had to get home before Annie did, or there'd be shit in the soup the next day. The other one was kidding him about Annie and trying to talk him into some pig feet and another beer at the cafe. It sounded so real that I believed it, but I kept my eye on the one in the street. He was edging toward my car, but that seemed normal enough because he was waiting for a spurt of traffic to go by. Watching that one was my mistake. The other one, the one who was insisting that he had to get home before Annie, whipped open the door next to the sidewalk and eased into the seat beside me. He was carrying one of those nickel-plated .32's, the ones we called Saturday Night Specials. They weren't much good, but they'd kill you from a couple of feet away.

"Sit still, white ass," he said.

I sat still.

The one still outside stopped pretending he was trying to cross to the cafe and circled the car. He moved into the back seat, directly behind me. He leaned forward and hooked an arm around my neck. The hard hump of muscle in his forearm almost choked me. "See what he's carrying."

The black with the .32 found the slapjack on the seat and passed it back. "This on the seat." He patted me down and handed my wallet over the seat back.

As soon as the black with the .32 moved away from me and was ready, the arm slipped away from my throat. In the back seat he used a pencil flashlight to go through my wallet.

"Hardman," he said behind me, "I've heard of you. What's a cop doing in this part of town?"

I was going to let the mistake ride, but the black on the seat beside me knew better. "He ain't a cop any more. Got throwed off the force over a year ago."

"That so, Hardman?"

"Yes."

There went that small chance of immunity. If they thought I was a cop it might not get too rough. But now they knew better. If I'd been thrown off the force, it wouldn't bring much heat when something happened to me. The way I'd left, if anything happened to me they might even declare a paid holiday.

"Hardman, what you doing down here?"

"Working up nerve enough to go over and order some pig knuckles to go."

"That ain't the answer." The arm hooked around my throat again. "Ferd!"

Ferd, the one with the .32, shifted the gun to his left hand and drove his right into my kidney. I wanted to scream, but the hump of muscle choked it off. There was nothing else to do, so I farted.

"Jesus," Ferd said, "I think he shit his pants."

The arm slacked so I could breathe.

"Not yet," I said, "but you keep that up, and ..."

"I'll make it easy for you," the one in the back seat said, "You watching the white chick, huh?"

It was time to make my mind up. I'd probably piss blood in the morning, anyway. A few more blows in the kidney, and I'd end up pissing blood and tissue. It wasn't worth it.

5

"Yeah," I said.

"For yourself?"

"No, her daddy. He's worried about her."

"That cunt can take care of herself," Ferd said, laughing.

"Watch your mouth," the other black said.

Ferd clamped his mouth shut.

"Maybe you ought to back off from the job."

"I think I ought to," I said.

"We see you following the girl around again, it won't be just a talk."

"I'm off the job, as of now."

"That's a smart white ass." The arm tightened around my neck and I was pulled back and up, until I was out of my seat. Ferd worked me over, belly and kidneys and groin. I wanted to vomit, but it was backed up and choked off by the arm at my throat. It wasn't until they were through and I was slammed forward against the steering wheel that it came gushing out. It splattered all over my pants and shoes and the floorboards.

"Remember, Hardman."

From the headlights and the engine noises, I knew they'd left. It was half an hour before I could sit up. It was another ten or fifteen minutes before I felt strong enough to drive. I didn't think I could make it to my house, so I drove over to Hump's apartment. I leaned against the wall in the entrance hall and pressed the buzzer until Hump came down the stairs and got me.

I think I slept for a time in the tub. Then it was a struggle to straighten myself out, and a harder one to step from the tub onto the bath mat. I was shaking all over when I dried off, and got into one of Hump's oversized terry cloth robes. Before I left the bathroom, I tried to pull the plug and let the bath water out, but I found I couldn't lean over that far and had to leave it.

Hump was in the kitchen with a bottle of J&B. He got a glass for me, and I eased into a chair across from him. Hump's coal-black and six-six, and weighs on the order of two hundred and seventy.

He was a defensive end at Michigan State and later with Cleveland. In his fourth year of pro ball he tore up a knee and the operation didn't restore it all the way. He'd lost a lot of his speed and quickness, and pro ball was out. He drifted down to Atlanta and did some coaching at one of the small black colleges in town. He gave that up after a couple of years because the pay wasn't much. Now he did whatever came along. Dirty or clean, it didn't matter to him. Since I felt the same way the last year or so, it was a common bond of sorts.

I met Hump two years ago, while I was still on the force, working nights. I'd gone to check into a brawl that had been reported at the Blue Light. The fight was over when I got there. Three black studs were spread all over the floor and Hump, barely sweating, was seated at the bar drinking draft beer.

"Those boys tried to have some fun on me," Hump said.

It seemed that the shortest of the three had started it by looking up at Hump and asking how the weather was up there. Hump had spit in his eye and said that it was raining. That was when the fight broke out. From the way Hump looked, it hadn't been a long fight. I remembered Hump from a game I'd seen him play against the Falcons, and I had a beer with him while we waited for the paddy wagon. The nervous owner told the story the same way Hump did, and when the wagon came I sent the three busted-up studs off to jail. They didn't argue at all. Jail was better than staying in the bar where Hump was.

In the year since I'd been thrown off the force, Hump and I had worked a few deals together. When he needed money and I needed a back-up man, I'd call him. If I had a friend left in Atlanta, it was probably Hump. But I'd never said anything like that to him. There was always the chance that he didn't feel that way about me at all.

Hump poured me a shot of the J&B. "I looked in your car. The slapjack's gone. The wallet's there, but there's no money in it."

"There wasn't much to start with," I said. "Fifteen bucks maybe."

"I left the windows open to air it out," he said.

I sipped at the J&B.

"You want to look around for these boys?"

"Not tonight," I said. "Maybe not ever."

He nodded, like that made sense to him. "You owe me one bit of trim for the one you chased away."

My memory was a bit blurred. Then, with the time screwed up, like it had happened a week ago, I remembered the girl with frizzy blonde hair who'd peeped out of the bedroom when Hump carried me into the bathroom. She looked like a hippie chick from around the tight-squeeze area.

"I owe you one, then."

"One whiff of you," Hump said, "and she remembered she had to be home."

On my third drink, I felt good enough to stagger over to the phone and make two calls. The first one was to Arch Campbell. I told him I'd been called out of town suddenly and I wouldn't be able to follow up on the job. I let him know that all I'd found out was that she was hanging out in some pretty rough bars. He said he'd send me a check for the one day's work.

My second call was to Raymond Hutto at the Schooner Topless Bar. When Hump heard me ask for Raymond, he came over and stood just past my shoulder, listening.

All I said to Raymond was that I was available. He said for me to drop by the Schooner at three the next afternoon. He might have something for me by then.

Hump was waiting when I hung up.

"You doing anything the next day or so?" I asked.

"No."

"I thought we might make a run to New York."

"Hardman," he said, smiling, "that's as good as trim, any day."

CHAPTER TWO

Three days later, I caught the noon flight from Hartsfield to LaGuardia. My round-trip ticket scheduled a morning return flight two days later. Since it was Raymond's money I went first class, and had the two drinks of scotch that came with the seat, and took a nap until the plane went into its landing pattern. Hump was already in New York. He'd taken a flight that left Atlanta five hours earlier. Hump knew the drill we'd set up, and I felt a lot better knowing that Hump was in the background watching me.

The airport bus dropped me at Grand Central. I caught a cab to the Barclay Hotel, where a reservation had been made for me by Raymond. I cancelled the reservation, explaining that I'd be staying with friends instead. I put a five on the clerk.

"There might be a message for me."

There'd be another five for him if he'd take the message. Then I had a cab drop me at Sheridan Square. I waited in front of the United Cigar stand until Hump came by in a cab and picked me up.

"You sure all this shucking and jiving all over town is worth it?" he asked.

"So far it is."

"We'll see." Hump gave directions to the cabbie and he picked his way through the screwed-up streets of the Village and over into the East Village.

It was a three-flight walk-up, a studio apartment. Hump had a key. He knocked and, when there wasn't an answer, he opened the door and motioned me inside. "The trim must still be out buying groceries with Sweet Raymond's money."

The phone was in the bedroom, on the floor. I sat on the edge of the rumpled bed and lifted the phone to my knee. Hump came in and made a fuss over the bed covers, as if straightening up.

"That girl's not neat," he said.

I grinned at him, knowing, and dialed Eastern Airlines.

"Well, I had to wake her up," Hump said.

The reservation clerk found us a flight back to Atlanta at sixten the next morning. I made the reservations in my name and Hump's.

He watched me. "We change the drill this time?"

"Might as well." The times before, Hump had gone back on the flight just before mine. He'd wander around Hartsfield and, if the way seemed clear, he'd get my car from the parking lot and be waiting when I came out. With that drill established, I thought it was time to change, just in case somebody had worked out our pattern.

We were having a beer in the kitchen when Hump's trim came in with a double armful of grocery bags. The girl, Lena, seemed surprised that I was white, and her hello was a little choked. I understood it because I'd seen the newspapers and pamphlets stacked around the apartment. She just didn't like whites. There wasn't any reason she had to, but it was going to make for a long night. I resigned myself to it and drank my beer. Hump helped her put the groceries away. When she went into the bedroom he followed her and closed the door. I couldn't hear what Hump was saying, but he was saying most of it.

Hump came out first. He put on his topcoat. "I'm going down to the corner for a bottle of J&B."

Lena came out of the bedroom a few minutes after he left. She'd changed to jeans and a print shirt. She was a pretty little thing, with skin the color of aged ivory. For a long time she just looked at me, as if she wanted to say something but the words wouldn't come out. Then an "ah, shit!" exploded off her lips. "If Hump says you're all right, I guess you have to be."

When Hump came back grinning sheepishly, the static was gone and she was telling me how she had met Hump. It was a comic encounter between Hump, the predatory man, and Lena, the N.Y.U. graduate student, at a party in Harlem. While she acted out the parts, what he said and what she said, Hump sat on the arm of her chair and ran his hand lightly over her shoulders. Hump didn't say anything, so I told about my first meeting with him at the Blue Light. When I changed the three black studs to five, he gave me a slow, sleepy wink past her shoulder.

At six I called the Barclay and found I had a message. I left Hump and Lena watching TV. and caught a cab. I had the cabbie wait for me and went inside. I gave the clerk the other five and got a folded sheet of memo paper. There was nothing on it but a printed PLEASE CALL and a number. I used one of the pay phones in the lobby.

"Yeah?"

"Man here from out of town."

He said, "Wellington Cinema at ten, back row."

We both hung up at the same time.

Just before the cab reached the apartment, I told the cabbie to stop in front of a small bar. I hadn't been gone very long, and I wanted Hump and Lena to have some time to themselves. It was a shorter trip than usual, and there wasn't any reason to ruin Hump's fun.

Exactly at ten I bought a ticket at the Wellington Cinema. I stood in the aisle until my eyes were accustomed to the darkness. That took a minute or two. On the screen a young man was shaking his hard-on at a fat-assed young girl who seemed frightened of it. It was large enough to be frightening. The back row was empty except for a single man. He was eating popcorn, the popcorn box balanced across his knees on a Samsonite briefcase. I moved down the row and sat down next to him. He turned slowly to look at me. His mouth was stuffed, slobbering over the popcorn.

"I'm Hardman."

He nodded. "You look like your picture." He slid the briefcase from his knees and placed it on the floor between us. He choked down the mouthful of popcorn and leaned toward me. "I thought I'd better warn you. There have been two hijacks in the last month."

"I'm warned." I got out the envelope of cash and slapped it against his leg. His hand caught it. Without another word, he got up and moved away from me, down the row and out the opposite exit. I waited until I counted off a slow hundred, and then I went out too.

If it was going to happen at all, I knew that it would have to happen right away. They wouldn't want to take a chance on me getting too far away from the skin-movie house before they made their try. They might lose me, and New York was a great city to stay lost in.

The briefcase made me stand out. At ten o'clock at night, I had to be the only shit walking around with a Samsonite in his hand. That was what bothered me. What made me feel good was that Hump, looking like the drunkest black ever, was staggering along after me, hitting all the lamps and walls as he came. Lena was with him, acting out the suffering wife who was trying to get her bad-ass husband home.

I could hear her embarrassed whispering. "Ernie, please, come on. The police are going to get you if you don't walk right."

And his angry reply: "Fuck off, bitch."

"Ernie, please don't talk like that."

I might have enjoyed the game-play if two men hadn't stepped out of the dark doorway ahead of me and moved in my direction. They were both big studs, and I thought, *Oh, God!* and my beat-up body began to ache with the memory of what Ferd had done to it. Skin started to sting again and the kidney pulsed a bit to let me know it hadn't forgotten.

Hump, I was thinking, stop all that play-acting and pay some attention.

As the two men closed on me, they divided so that they had me flanked. The man on my left had a slick-smooth scar under his right eye and a mashed left ear. The man to my right was younger and hadn't been around long enough to show the mileage yet.

"Hardman?" the young one asked.

Before I could answer, I heard Lena raise her voice behind me. "Ernie, you slow down, you hear me?"

"Just one more drink," Hump said.

The older man, the one with the battered face, looked up at the voices and he began a smile, as if he was about to say something about drunk spades. At that moment, Hump barreled into him. I heard him grunt as the wind went out of him and he smacked the wall. The young man was stunned only for a split second, and then his hand went for his raincoat pocket. It never got there. I was that split second ahead of him, and had one of my hard-toed shoes back and ready. I kicked him in the shin hard enough to break the bone. I didn't hear it break because, by the time it landed, Hump was through with the first man. He lunged past me and a black hand about the size of a ham hit the man on the side of his head. He went down fast and bounced off the side of a car fender. Just to be sure, I stepped forward and kicked him once in the balls.

A block away, I flagged down a cab. Lena wasn't over the shock yet. I could feel her trembling next to me. Hump put an arm around her and whispered in her ear. "There wasn't no reason to worry. Those were real candy-asses."

On the way back to Lena's apartment, we changed cabs twice. Hump thought it was a lot of trouble for nothing, but he didn't say so. He knew it was the drill. No matter what happened, we followed the drill.

We got back to the apartment in time for the evening news. Lena fixed us a late snack, and Hump got out the J&B. It was a long wait until the time to leave for the airport. Lena and Hump went into the bedroom, and I settled down to watch a couple of the late movies.

Around four the next morning, Lena called us a cab. I waited outside in the hall while they said their good-byes. I gave her a little wave, and we went downstairs to wait for the cab. A few minutes later, we were on our way to LaGuardia.

"You think it's done?" Hump asked.

I nodded. "It was probably that shit in the movie house. Wanted to sell it twice. Wanted Raymond's money and somebody else's."

Hump looked at the briefcase. "It's already high enough."

I looked at Hump then, to see if he was taking some of that high moral tone that the anti-drug workers had. He wasn't. It was just a flat statement on the price of smack. He'd gone past that now, and he was grinning to himself, as if remembering something that had happened during the day between him and his New York City trim.

It was a slow morning at Hartsfield International. The cleanup crews were working their way through the coffee cups, Kleenex, and candy wrappers when we passed through. I got my car from the parking lot, and Hump drove back into town and out West Peachtree until we reached the Southern Peachtree Arms. It was still early, and the security man at the door didn't want to bother Mr. Hutto. I kept pushing him until he did. Raymond sounded sleepy and a little pissed when he told the security man to send us on up. He opened the door as soon as we touched the buzzer.

Raymond Hutto was swarthy and very short. It wasn't until I saw him in his robe and slippers that I realized he probably wore elevator shoes. The other times I'd seen him he'd looked about two inches taller. I guess they don't make bedroom slippers that give the same kind of illusion.

He nodded at us, and we followed him back into the kitchen. A kettle of water was just beginning to stir over the gas burner. I put the briefcase on the kitchen table and Raymond brought out a key from the pocket of his robe. Hump and I stood around and watched while he opened one of the flat plastic bags and tasted a pinch of the smack. He made a face and looked over at me.

"You're not due for a couple of days."

"I know when I'm due," I said.

"Any trouble?"

"Some, but none that mattered." I indicated Hump. "That's why he's with me."

He closed the briefcase and locked it. "Wait here." He took the briefcase into the bedroom and closed the door behind him.

"Some place," Hump said.

I agreed. The kettle began to whistle, and I found the right knob and turned off the flame under it.

Raymond returned a few minutes later with a sheaf of bills. He counted them out to me. Then, while Raymond watched, I counted the money into two equal shares.

"Equal split?" Raymond asked.

I nodded and handed Hump his share. Raymond followed us to the door. At the door I turned back to him. "Somebody tried to hijack us half a block from the pickup point where I made the buy. No proof, but I think it was the bastard who passed the stuff to me."

"I'll send the word up to New York," Raymond said.

"Right or wrong, if I see that shit again I'm going to break his head."

"We have ways of finding out." Raymond opened the door for us.

We went out into the hallway and he closed the door behind us.

I stopped in front of the building where Hump's apartment is. He hesitated, with his hand on the door. "What was that shit about the equal shares?"

I kept my face straight and shook my head. "Don't know."

"Come on, you know."

"Raymond just found out you're not my spade flunky."

"Does it matter to him?"

"Maybe. Maybe not."

Hump grinned. "It might mean you don't show the proper leadership qualities." He opened the door and got out.

"Get some sleep."

"Let's get piss-assed later," he said.

I told him to call me when he woke up.

I drove on home. Home is a falling-down old house about twenty minutes or so out of the city. It needs a new paint job, and half the time there's trouble with the plumbing. For all that, it belongs to me and the mortgage man. I'd started buying it a year and a half ago, when I'd first got the bright idea to marry Marcy. When that blew up, I'd kept on making the payments because it wasn't much more expensive than making rent payments. There's a front lawn I don't keep up, and a big backyard where I can sit in the spring and summer and drink beer and watch the seasons

ATLANTA DEATHWATCH

pass. Liking nature is one way of numbing the mind against all the other things it wants to worry about.

I got the *Constitution* from the bushes beside the front steps and the quart of milk from next to the door and went inside. As soon as I was inside, I knew something was wrong. I wanted to step back, but it was too late. Ferd, from in front of the Dew Drop In a few nights before, stepped from behind the door and placed the Saturday Night Special on a line with my nose.

"The Man wants to see you."

"Look," I said, "I quit working that job."

Another black, perhaps the one from the back seat, came out of the kitchen with a half-eaten sandwich in his hand. He took the milk from me and carried it into the kitchen. I heard the refrigerator door open and slam shut. He returned and stood on the other side of me.

"My car or yours?" I asked.

"Mine," Ferd said.

I tossed the newspaper on the sofa, and the other black patted me down while Ferd kept the gun on me. Then we went outside and got into a black Ford that was parked half a block down the road.

17

CHAPTER THREE

The boarded-up building was just off Whitehall, only a few blocks from the service station where Emily Campbell had stopped for gas and made her phone calls. The building looked like it was about half a step from Urban Renewal. The chipping paint above the boarded windows advertised auto parts for cars, trucks and buses. That must have been a long time ago. Ferd parked in the dirt lot next to it, and we got out. They led me around to the back of the building. The other black unlocked a door there, and Ferd motioned me inside.

The stairs we went up were old and creaky, but they'd been swept and scrubbed recently. Before I reached the door at the top of the stairs, Ferd pushed me to one side. He tapped lightly on the door with the butt of his Saturday Night Special. The door swung open.

I wasn't prepared for what I saw. After the bleak ugliness of the outside, it looked like a palace. But it was a palace designed by someone who couldn't see the colors, or didn't care. There were deep red carpets and silver walls and a flat black ceiling. There was a polished round brass bar in the center of the room, with enough booze on the tiered shelves to open for business at lunch time downtown. Over to the right, the sofa and chairs picked up the brass tone. Straight ahead, beyond this room, I could see a kitchen with enough gleaming gadgets to satisfy almost any housewife.

The black who opened the door motioned me inside. From behind, Ferd gave me a push. I took a couple of steps into the room, turned, and faced him. Ferd indicated the bar. "Want a drink, Hardman?"

"It's a little early," I said.

Ferd played it up for the other two. "That's not what I heard. Heard drinking was why you ain't on the force any more."

"That was some other vice," I said.

"Fat little boys?" Ferd laughed and the other two joined him, and then the door beside the sofa opened and all the laughing broke off.

The man who entered was around thirty. His skin was coal black and had the hard shine and glisten of agate. He looked as lean and hard as a rake handle. He wore a pair of trousers, shirt and tie and a quilted smoking jacket. As soon as I saw him, I thought, *Oh, God! He didn't see enough Westerns when he was a little boy. His mother took him to those godawful English drawing room comedies instead.* And when he spoke it was with a precision that I felt he'd learned from records played on a turntable that was a few revolutions too slow.

"Mr. Hardman, won't you have a seat?"

I stepped past him and sat on the sofa.

"Have you been offered something to drink?"

Before I could answer, Ferd said, "He said it was too early for him."

"Then a cup of coffee perhaps?"

I nodded. "Coffee's fine."

"The Kenya coffee," he said to Ferd. "The new shipment."

Ferd went into the kitchen and, a few seconds later, I heard the electric coffee grinder going.

"I prefer African coffee to South American."

"I'm used to instant," I said.

"Then you will notice the difference." He offered me a cigarette from a box on the coffee table in front of the sofa, and I took one. "My own blend," he said. One of the other blacks leaned forward and lit them for us.

I took a couple of puffs and said they were very good, very different. I could see that we were running out of social things to do. Sooner or later, we'd have to get down to the business that had brought me here.

"I assume you're wondering why I asked you to drop by?"

"I don't remember being asked," I said.

He laughed, like a good host trying to make me feel at home. "I think Ferd was afraid you might decline, after your long trip up North."

So he knew about that. "Since I'm here I don't mind talking, but I'd like to know who I'm talking to."

"They call me The Man. My own name isn't that impressive." He looked at me questioningly. "I thought in your years with the police, you might have heard of me."

"I guess I did. But I didn't know there was just one The Man in town." I could remember the times when someone we'd arrest would say something about The Man, but I'd just assumed it was a black way of saying The Boss, or The Man I Work For.

"Have you seen today's paper?"

"Not yet."

"I thought you hadn't. Otherwise you might have been more reluctant to drop by." He held out his hand and one of the blacks put the front section of the *Constitution* in it. He passed it over to me.

It was hard to miss. It was the big cover story with a picture. *Tech Co-ed Murdered.* The story below the picture and headline said that Emily Campbell, a sophomore at Georgia Tech, had been found with her neck broken in her Toyota in a downtown parking lot. The rest of the story was vague, as if they didn't have many facts because the body had been found not long before the paper had to go to press.

I folded the paper and handed it back to him. I waited, trying to show an outward calm I didn't feel.

"Of course," The Man said, "I know where you were." He dropped the paper on the floor. "You were the first one I looked for when I heard about it."

That sounded reasonable. "I quit the job the night I met your friends. I try to take good advice."

"Raymond and I do business now and then. My information said that you'd been seen with him. He was kind enough to tell me you were out of town and where you'd gone. And he was kind enough to call me when he knew you were back."

I thought back over the meeting with Raymond. I remembered that he'd been in the bedroom long enough to call The Man and say I was back from New York.

The Man was reading my mind. "I told him it was important. I wanted you for a job."

Raymond hadn't said anything about it to me because it was business between The Man and me. It wasn't his concern at all. Raymond never liked to hang around the fringes of other people's business. It got you noticed if the business went bad for some reason or other.

Ferd came in with the coffee pot and two cups on a tray. He put the tray on the copper bar and poured it there. He brought it to us black. The Man waited until I sipped at mine, watching me.

"It's excellent." The coffee had a delicate quality that I'd never tasted in coffee before.

"I thought you'd appreciate it. I have a few pounds flown in every month or so." The Man sipped at his coffee and put it aside. "I think we can talk business now."

"I'm not sure what business we have."

"Let me be honest with you. I have to admit a mistake. If I hadn't forced you off the job, Emily might still be alive. And even if she were dead, we might know who had done it."

I kept my face as bland and hard as I could. "What was Emily Campbell to you?" Out of the corner of my eye, I could see Ferd leaning away from the bar toward me.

The Man noticed him also. He shook his head at Ferd and then faced me once more. "I loved her." It came out as if he hadn't been thinking when he answered, almost like a reflex.

"That would make you the number-one boy, if the police knew about it."

"You know and my associates know." His voice flattened out. "My associates won't talk."

"There might be letters in her room, notes from you," I said.

"No letters, no notes."

"A diary?"

"Not that I know of."

That wasn't going anywhere. I asked how he'd met her.

Just a few months before, during the summer, Emily Campbell had been working with one of the social action groups that was trying to increase black voter registration. One afternoon she'd stopped The Man and asked if he was registered to vote. The Man had said he wasn't, and he wasn't interested. She'd pursued him down the street.

"How will you get your rights if you don't vote?"

"I don't need that kind of rights," he'd answered.

She wouldn't give up and, to prove his point, he'd taken her to the apartment and shown her how he lived. That had stunned her for a time, but it hadn't stopped her. Very well, so he did have the creature comforts (yes, she'd used those words) but what about the rest of his race? Didn't he want the rest of his people to enjoy the same things?

"Let them scratch for it," he'd said.

When she left after an hour, he thought he was through with her, but he wasn't. She came back the next day and the day after that. Finally, to get rid of her, he'd registered. But that wasn't all she wanted; now she wanted him to use his influence to convince other blacks to register. As the days went by, something else was happening to the two of them. It was something he didn't want to happen, and some hard part of him told him to go ahead and do her white ass, if that was what she was offering him. It might be a way of burning off the fever she'd put in him. But it hadn't been that way at all. Instead, the fever had increased. And, because he was an honest man with himself, he had to admit that he loved her, and that was all there was to that. It had been great, it had been wonderful, until the night he found out that Hardman was watching her. And now, four days later, she was dead in a parking lot.

"I don't see where I fit into this," I said.

"I asked around about you. Here and there. I've heard the good and the bad. I don't mind the kind of bad I heard. It's the kind that I understand. The good I've heard is the kind of good that I understand." He stood up and reached into the front pocket of his trousers. He brought out a thick wad of money and counted off five hundred-dollar bills. "I want you to poke around in it and find out the truth."

I didn't touch the money. "The police might find the killer, and then you're out money."

He shook his head. "You know how many killings there were in Atlanta this year? Almost one a day. And a hell of a lot of them are not solved."

"If I work for you, I work without any help from your boys."

"That's agreed."

"You know Hump Evans. He works with me."

The Man spread the wad of cash and put down two more hundreds. When he stopped I shook my head. "Hump costs the same as I do." The Man put down three more bills and stuck the wad away. I folded the bills and put them in my shirt pocket. "That buys you eight or ten day's work. If I don't have something by then, I probably never will."

"If you need more, stop by."

I drained off the last of my coffee and stood up. "I have a friend left on the force. I'll start with what the police have." I moved toward Ferd with the cup and saucer in my left hand.

"Your methods are left up to you," The Man said.

I moved a step closer to the bar. I was between The Man and Ferd. "There is just one thing more. Since I'm working for you, I don't have to take any more shit off the other help, do I?"

The Man blinked, as if he didn't understand what I was asking.

"I mean, I can have my balls back, can't I?"

"Certainly, Hardman, I don't see. ..."

Without looking at Ferd, as if there was still one more thing I wanted to get straight with The Man, I handed Ferd the cup and saucer. He was listening, as if he wasn't sure where all this was going either. Taking the cup and saucer from me was just a reflex. But as soon as he had it, I whirled toward him, ducked one shoulder, and hit him in the balls as hard as I could. The cup and saucer went flying over the bar. Ferd let out a scream and fell against the bar. The glasses and bottles rattled, and he turned in his fall and curled up, clutching his groin. I leaned over him and jerked the .32 out of his waistband. I tossed it on the sofa next to The Man. Then I turned back to him and kicked him in the stomach as hard as I could. In the heat of it, I considered one more kick, this time to the ribs, but I held up. I backed away, watching The Man and the other two blacks.

"My car smells like vomit." I took a deep breath. "Now I'm even."

The Man nodded. He could understand that.

I went outside and down the steps before I remembered that I didn't have my car with me. I wasn't about to go back up those stairs and ask for a lift. I walked over to Whitehall, caught a cruising cab and gave him Hump's address

CHAPTER FOUR

The sofa wasn't that comfortable. Around four that afternoon, I gave up and wrote off last night's sleep as a total loss. I rattled around in the kitchen until Hump heard me. It took half an hour of really trying before Hump came out of the bedroom, looking mean and puffy around the eyes.

"You ever spend any time at home?"

"Not lately," I said.

"Maybe you ought to consider it." He got a beer out of the refrigerator and opened it. He went into the bathroom, and the shower ran a long time. When he came back into the kitchen he was still puffy, but the bad mood was gone. He dropped the empty beer bottle into a trash bag and got down the J&B and a glass. As he poured he said, "That's some job you picked for us."

"It's better than being unemployed."

"You sure?"

I wasn't. If it was a sex crime or one of those kook crimes, then the victim probably didn't know the one who committed it. If there was no previous relationship between the murderer and Emily Campbell, then you had something over a million and a half suspects, and no special place to begin. Those were long, long odds.

"It came as a Crackerjack prize," I said.

While Hump dressed, I got Art Maloney at his home number. He sounded surprised to hear from me. It had been some time. And when I suggested supper at the Mandarin he said he could meet us there in forty-five minutes.

Our drink refills about the same time Art did. He was wearing that same dark suit with the shiny seat that he'd been wearing for the last five or six years. He and Edna had to cut corners to feed and clothe the four kids, and that didn't leave much for new suits to replace worn-out ones. His hair was a little thinner now, but the flat Irish face looked about the same as it had when we'd shared a patrol car, back when we'd both been starting out.

He settled for a beer because he had to go on shift later. While he sipped it, he spent a long time trying to decide what to order. Maybe he thought it was Dutch, and wanted to order what he could afford. I didn't want to embarrass him, so I told a story about losing a bet to Hump. The whole supper, drinks and all, were on me. When that was settled, we ordered enough food to feed a small Chinese village.

While we were working over the egg rolls, the roast pork and the spare ribs, I decided I might as well begin. "You working on the Emily Campbell thing?"

Art blinked over that. "Yeah."

"I've got a slight interest in it. Did some work for her father once."

Hump jumped in. "The write-up in the paper didn't tell much."

"Wasn't much to tell," Art said. Then he went on to tell us everything he knew. She'd left her dorm at Tech at five, give or take a few minutes. She didn't tell anyone where she was going. A few minutes after midnight, a wino who was cold and looking for a place to sleep, after watching the Toyota for an hour or so, opened the back door and found the body. It scared him so much that he'd dropped his pint bottle of Rocket and broken it. With the evening a complete loss, the wino had turned into a good citizen and flagged down a patrol car.

Art stopped talking while the waitress brought out the covered main dishes.

"Time of death?" I asked.

Art shrugged. "As close as we can figure, maybe ten."

"Killed somewhere else?"

Art nodded. "We think so. Strangled, her neck broken. Probably dumped in the back seat, and car driven to the downtown parking lot and left. No one saw it get there, and there don't seem to be any prints so far that mean much."

"Robbery?"

"Not likely." Art helped himself to the rice and spooned some sweet-and-sour pork over it. "Purse in the back seat with some cash in it, about what she usually carried. A number of credit cards, all there."

Hump motioned toward the shrimp in lobster sauce. Art passed it to him.

"Rape?"

"I think we're supposed to believe that. Girl's underpants torn off, scratches on the legs."

"Why not?" I asked.

"No sperm on the outside of her or inside her."

Hump asked why that meant anything.

"Maybe it doesn't," Art said.

"Sperm makes a better rape case," I said. "Not much doubt then. Without it, it might just be a show of some kind, a way of trying to send you off in the wrong direction."

"I might be just doing a lot of hoping," Art said. "Not that much to back it up, not so far."

I explained it to Hump. "If it's not a sex crime, a nut crime, then it was probably committed by someone Emily Campbell knew, and it was probably committed for some reason that Art can dig out."

"Given time," Art said.

"And luck," I said.

Art had played our game long enough. "What's your real interest in this, Hardman?"

"Like I told you. Also, I saw the girl once. She seemed like a nice kid."

"That's as far as I've gone, too. Nice, bright kid."

"A big waste," I said, and we all shook our heads sadly and went on eating Chinese food.

When the waitress was up front with the check and the bills I'd given her, I wadded up a fifty and stuffed it into Art's suit coat pocket. He knew what I was doing but pretended that he didn't, and Hump pretended that he hadn't noticed, either. It was hard on Art, but I knew he needed the money. I guess he could convince himself that it wasn't like "taking" out on the street. Both of us knew, I guess, that it was just a short-term loan.

"You feel like protecting your old white buddy?"

We were on the way back from the Mandarin, heading through the downtown part of town. The weather was changing now, getting colder, and the wind was in swirls of dirt and trash.

"What you have in mind, old white buddy?"

"A beer in the Dew Drop In Cafe," I said.

Hump gave it a bit of time, as if he were considering it from all the possible angles. "A deal," he said, "if you'll take me to some redneck hog wallow and protect me some night."

"Pick your hog wallow," I said, but I sounded a lot more sure than I felt.

You could hear the neon sign buzzing and humming from across the street. We crossed the street together. I pulled up just outside the closed door and said, "You first."

Hump pushed the door open and leaned in. At first they didn't see me behind him. The three blacks at the bar looked him over and then started to ease their looks away. But then I was uncovered, and their eyes whipped back at me. The bartender saw me and moved toward the end of the bar nearest us. Besides the three blacks at the bar, one booth to the left of us was occupied with construction workers. Their hard hats were on the floor outside the booth.

Hump moved toward the bartender. He was big, with round, thick shoulders and an oily-looking knife scar that began somewhere under the edge of his t-shirt and ran around the left side of his neck. "Gentlemen, I'm sorry, but we don't serve whites in here."

Down the bar, past another black, the big stud with the Afro, from a few nights before, leaned forward and asked, "What you sirring him for, Ad?" Hump turned very slowly and looked at him. He didn't say anything. He just looked. Even when the stud with the Afro looked away he wasn't through. He was just waiting to see what happened next.

I said it loud enough so the blacks at the bar could hear me, too. "You got a phone?"

The bartender nodded.

"Call The Man and tell him Hardman's here and wants to ask some questions, but that you don't feel like answering them."

"I don't know anybody with that name."

"Sure you do." I remembered the beating out in the car, delivered by Ferd. "You've called him at least once before." I stepped up onto one of the stools. "Now draw me a beer and go call The Man."

While he was drawing the beer I could see his lips moving. The stud with the big Afro wasn't convinced, but he wasn't arguing much, either. Ad, the bartender, brought us the draft beers and then ducked under the bar to the pay phone in back. Hump and I drank our beers and looked at each other, and very carefully avoided looking anywhere else. A minute or so later, Ad came back from the phone looking like he'd been lightly burned by The Man. He nodded at the big Afro once, and then he reached us, he nodded. "He says I should answer all your questions."

"Four nights ago there was a white girl in here."

"Yeah," he said, "I remember."

"How long did she stay?"

"Eleven or so."

"What did she do while she was here?" I pushed my empty glass toward him.

"Drank some beer, played the juke box some." He took my empty glass and Hump's down to the tap and refilled them. He put them down in front of us. "And she kept making phone calls."

"Was she calling The Man?"

He thought a minute. "I don't know, but I don't think so. He had business that night, and he called me and said the girl was coming by, and for me to look out for her. He said he'd send for her when his business was over."

"You got any idea who she was calling?"

"Johnny might." Ad tipped his head in the direction of the stud with the big Afro.

"See if he'll have a beer with us."

Johnny came reluctantly. He wanted everybody in the bar to know that he wasn't in the least bit of a hurry. He put his elbows on the bar next to Hump and looked at the fresh beer as if it were piss or worse. "You want something?"

Ad asked the question for me. "The white girl in here four nights ago. You know who she was talking to on the phone?"

"I wasn't studying any white cunt."

Ad grinned at me. "He was trying to make some time. He was trying to mess with her some while she was at the phone. He was going a little strong, so I had to have a word with him."

"How was I to know she was The Man's private stuff? She looked like plain white ass to me."

"You hear anything of what she said on the phone?" This from Hump.

"She said something like, 'Eddie, Eddie, I don't want you to do that.'"

"You sure it was Eddie?" I asked.

He nodded toward me. "I'm sure."

"How'd she sound?"

"Like she was begging," he said.

"That's all?"

"Whoever Eddie was, I think that stud hung up on her. She got this puzzled look on her face and called his name a time or two more, and then she hung up herself."

I thanked him, and he gave me the barest of nods and went back over to his seat. "She leave with The Man that night?" I asked Ad.

"I don't think so. You see, he called a few minutes after she left and wanted to talk to her, but she wasn't around."

"She leave by herself?"

"Nobody in here left with her, if that's what you mean."

"Maybe she drove over to see The Man," I said.

"If you know anything at all," Ad said, "then you know it don't take long to get there from here." He emptied the ashtray in front of us. "Not ten minutes, anyway, and that's how long she was gone when he called."

I wanted to pay for the beer, but Ad wouldn't take the money. So I left a couple of dollars anyway, and said he could let Johnny have a free ride for a glass or two.

Hump got the car turned around and headed for my house. "Eddie. That's your man, huh?"

"It either fits in somewhere, or it doesn't."

Hump grunted. It didn't sound like agreement. "Three days before the murder. That's a thin tie."

"The Man was going with her, and he said he didn't kill her. Right at the moment, that doesn't leave anybody."

"A sex nut, maybe," Hump said.

"At that gas station she made three calls. One might have been to The Man. That leaves two calls."

"It might have taken three calls to find The Man."

"Or she called a couple of places trying to find Eddie. I wonder who the hell Eddie is."

"Eddie Fisher. Eddie LeBaron. Fast Eddie Felson."

He went on naming Eddies until we reached my driveway.

I got up at nine and had coffee and toast, and dressed in my best Brooks Brothers suit. It was one of those white-gray overcast mornings that looked like snow but usually wasn't in Atlanta. I pointed for the gold dome of the Capitol and worked my way across town. I found a parking space about five blocks away and walked it.

Some time later I was getting a hand-shake and a backslap from Hugh Muffin. It was just routine, but he did it so well that sometimes you forgot. He really acted like seeing you made his day. I suspected he'd do the same with an investigator from Internal Revenue. But under that potbelly and friendly Uncle Hugh exterior, there was a ridge of sharp steel about two feet wide.

It was time to get down to business. "Bad thing about the Campbell girl." I said.

He set his face in the sad, funereal look. "Arch's broken up. His only child, you know."

"Is he still in town?"

"He was yesterday."

"I'd like to talk to him," I said, "but I'm not sure he'd see me."

"The guilties, huh?" He pursed his mouth as if he were about to spit out some tobacco juice. "To tell the truth, boy, he was a bit pissed at you … at first. He seemed to believe that Emily'd still be alive if you'd done the job you'd agreed to. It took some talking. Lord, I did some real talking before he admitted that you couldn't watch her twenty-four hours a day, and if somebody wanted to kill her, they could always find a time and a place."

"Maybe we could work a swindle," I said.

"Love those," he said.

"I've got a client who wants me to look into the murder but doesn't want to be known." I was watching him, and I could see the foxy slipping in. "You knew Emily pretty well, didn't you?"

"She was like my own child."

"Then he'd believe you if you told him that you'd hired me to look around for a few days."

"He might."

"Also, I could drop your name here and there, and it might give me a bit of clout when I need it."

"Who's your client?" he asked.

"I can't say right now."

"But you'll tell me later, huh?"

I said I would. He got up and got his topcoat. As he struggled into it, he said, "Might as well seem to be spending money in a good cause when it really doesn't cost me anything." He switched out the light and locked the outer door. "But you're using my name, son, and I'd better not find out that I'm the one being swindled."

Hugh didn't bother with ringing the room from the Regency lobby. We rode the glass-bubble elevator to the ninth floor and walked around the narrow, terrace-like hallway until we reached 922. Before he knocked, Hugh motioned me out of the doorway sightline.

I sat on a bench and smoked a cigarette. Almost five minutes later by my watch, the door opened again and Hugh said, "Come in, Mr. Hardman." There were two men in the room besides Hugh Muffin. Arch Campbell sat on the edge of the nearest twin bed, rigid and hard-backed, as if Hugh had seated him there. His face was almost blue with anger and his lips were trembling.

"Mr. Hardman, just because....I don't want you to think, just because I agreed to..."

I said I understood.

The other man stood in the far rear corner of the room. He was talking softly into the telephone. His face was turned away from me at first, but I could see the blue-black hair worn long and the dark, sun-tanned neck and tanned hand that held the receiver. When he finished and hung up and faced me, I could read in his hard mouth that he wasn't one of the friendly people.

Hugh said, "This is Ben Coleman, Arch's business manager."

I put out a hand as he stepped toward me, but he ignored it and leaned over Arch Campbell. "They're sending up coffee," he said.

I looked over my hand to see if it was especially dirty, and then put a cigarette in it and lit it. Ben Coleman, after Campbell nodded, straightened up and looked at me. "I was against using you, all along."

I didn't say anything. I just waited.

"If you'd been there when...." Arch Campbell began.

Hugh sat on the twin bed next to him and put an arm around his shoulders. "Arch, this isn't getting us anywhere."

"Hugh, goddammit...oh, all right." He braced himself. "What do you want to know, Mr. Hardman?"

"When I had you call your daughter, did you talk about anything else?"

"I didn't talk to her."

"You didn't...?"

"Her line was busy. When I called back a few minutes later, she wasn't there."

That was a possibility I hadn't considered. When Emily Campbell had run out of the dorm that evening looking frightened, it wasn't because her father had said he was coming over. It was some other cause that flushed her out into my tail. I ran the film-like memory of that first time I'd seen Emily Campbell, fighting the sweater to get her arms into the sleeves, burning rubber as she left the parking lot. It was a kind of panic that a visit from a father shouldn't cause. But the facts I'd had at the time had forced me to read it that way.

"I tried your home number several times," Arch Campbell said, "but you weren't there, and when you called later that night, I'd had a few drinks and I forgot…"

"Did you see her after that night?"

"No. I sent Ben but…"

Ben Coleman jumped in. "I spent half the next day trying to find her. I drew a blank, all the way." He looked at Arch. "Maybe I should have kept trying."

Arch shook his head. "There wasn't any way we could know."

"I'd like to look through her belongings, out at Tech," I said.

"The police already have," Arch said.

"I'd like to look for myself."

Hugh stood up. "I hired Hardman. The least we can do is help him cut a few corners."

"My sister, Carrie Nesbitt, is going over to the dormitory late this afternoon to pack up her things." He looked at his watch. "You could meet her there at four o'clock."

"I'd rather go sooner than that."

He pushed himself up from the bed and walked to the phone. "I'll call the housemother and tell her I'm sending you over."

"That would be better for me," I said.

While he made the call, the other three of us looked at the walls and the ceiling. Hugh still had his topcoat on, and he was worrying one of the leather buttons. Ben Coleman, angry and sullen, smoked a cigarette in short puffs. Besides the anger and frustration, there was the stuff of grief in the room, and I wanted to get out into Atlanta's wind and dirt and pollution. But I had one more question to ask.

Arch Campbell put the phone down and turned back to me. "Ask for Mrs. Peterson. She's expecting you."

Now my question. "Do you know anybody named Eddie who might have been a friend of Emily's?"

"I don't think so." He spread his hands helplessly. "I didn't know any of her Atlanta friends."

On the way out, I passed the waiter bringing in a tray of coffee.

"Man on the hall!" Mrs. Peterson's shout was followed by a few giggles and squeals. Her already sour mouth turned down more at the corners. Down the hall, a few heads popped out of doorways, looked at us, and then darted out of sight. I guess I wasn't the man they were looking for.

Mrs. Peterson unlocked the door with her master key and let me in. "The police have already been here."

"I'm not the police," I said. "Just a friend of the family."

That didn't completely satisfy her. While she searched for another approach, she opened the drapes and let in the pale December light.

It was like a hundred thousand other college rooms. The standard impersonality softened somewhat by prints and posters and the drapes that mother had had especially made for it. There were two single beds, two desks with small bookcases above, and two straight-backed chairs. One bed was still covered with a bright red bedspread. The other bed had been stripped and the mattress folded.

"Did Emily have the room to herself?"

"Why, no." The thin lashes blinked at me. "Marcia, her roommate, after we heard the news, moved in with another girl down the hall. She couldn't bear to be alone in the room ... after what happened."

"Is Marcia here now?"

"She's still in class."

"I'd like to talk to her."

She started for the door. "I'll leave a note in her mailbox. They all check their mail this time of day."

"Thank you, Mrs. Peterson."

As soon as she cleared the doorway I closed the door after her.

I worked the closet first. It was just a habit of mine. One day, on a suicide investigation with Art Maloney, kidding, I'd said that you could tell a lot about a person from the trash and odds and ends that collect in his clothing. So far I hadn't proven it, but I kept trying. This time wasn't very different. I went through every piece of clothing in the closet and every pocket. When I was done, I had a half pack of stale Winstons, a stub to a Falcon game and a Hawk game, some graying wads of unused and slightly used Kleenex, seven jagged halves of movie tickets, a paper clip, a felt-tipped pen with a chewed cap and a note, probably passed in class, that asked Emily if she wanted to have lunch after class. The note was signed with a big *M*.

From the closet I went to the dresser. The top drawer held stockings and socks. That stopped me, and I went back to the closet and opened the door again. There, hanging on the inside of the door, was one of those shoe bag affairs with about ten pairs of shoes in the pockets. I took out each shoe, felt inside it, and then felt down in the pocket. On the second row, four pockets over, I felt a lump and worked it out. It was a wad of tinfoil. When I unfolded the tinfoil I found about a quarter-ounce of grass and a lump of hash. I put that in my coat pocket and hoped I didn't get arrested for a traffic violation on the way home. The other shoes and pockets added nothing else to my collection.

When the dresser blanked me, too, I moved on to the book-case. I took out each book and shook it over the desk. I found a lot of place markers and notes, but nothing else. I was picking through the single desk drawer when the door opened behind me.

A dark-haired young girl stood in the doorway. She was around five-feet-two, and a bit on the chubby side. But the breasts must have been real, from the way she carried them—as if they were her best feature, with all the built-in arrows pointing their way. She held a piece of paper in one hand. She looked at it, and then at me.

"You're Mr. Hardman?"

I nodded.

"I'm Marcia Trusdall."

I motioned to a chair on the bare side of the room. She sat down carefully and made a big gesture of making sure that her short skirt didn't show me much. "I really don't have much time."

"It won't take long." I offered her a cigarette, but she preferred her own, a menthol brand, and I played the gentleman and lit it for her. "How long have you known Emily?"

"Since September, a year ago. We roomed together all last year and this year, until now."

"You get along pretty well?"

"She was my best friend, but…" She checked herself and looked at me, to see if I was going to help her through it. When I didn't, she said, "Maybe I shouldn't say this about her."

"Anything you say stops here."

"Well, the last few months, since we started this year, she hasn't been the same."

"How?"

"We didn't spend any time together. She was like…well, always charging out at all hours, without telling me where she was going. The times I've had to lie for her, saying she was at the library when I didn't know where she was!"

"It sounds like a man, to me," I said.

"I thought so, too." She'd tired of the cigarette. She stubbed it out in the ashtray on the bare desk behind her. "But it wasn't a college boy." That gave her an idea and she looked at me closely, but I could see I didn't measure up very well. "I think it was an older man."

"Is that right?"

"Maybe even a married man."

I gave her my best disbelieving stare. "No?"

"It would have to be, to explain all that happened this year. We were such good friends, and then, for no reason at all, we were walking around each other, like we were just strangers." She sighed. "To tell the truth, I was looking for a neat way of moving out on her. It was getting on my nerves."

I said I could certainly understand how she felt. That reassured her, and she smiled and arranged her skirt once more. "Did she ever talk to you about somebody named Eddie?"

"No, I don't think so." She hesitated. "Unless it was …"

"Yeah?"

"Well, a year ago, we were joking around one night, and we were talking about the first boy we'd been in love with. I'd told her about mine, a basketball player three years ahead of me in high school. Emily started to tell me about hers, a boy named Eddie she'd been in love with when she was sixteen, and then Cynthia, from down the hall, came in to borrow my typewriter, and I never heard the rest of it."

"It's odd that you remember the name at all."

"I wouldn't, not really, except for the fact that she got a phone call one night. That was last spring, and I was here alone. The man said he was just passing through town, and didn't have a phone number to leave for her to return the call. I think he would have hung up, but I asked him what his name was." She gave me a smile that seemed to apologize for being young. "You see, it's almost a written law that, when somebody calls up, you just *have* to get his name. No matter what you have to do." She laughed. "You wouldn't believe how shy some of these boys are! They finally work up nerve enough to call you, and if you're not there, they might not call back."

I said it wasn't so different with older people.

"He didn't give me a last name. He said just to tell her Eddie, and that she'd know who he was, that he was an old, old friend."

"How did Emily act when you told her about the call?"

"She didn't say anything. She said, 'Oh?' and went off to take a shower."

"And that was while you were still talking to each other?" I asked.

"Yes."

I thanked her, and walked to the door with her, and let her out. She went off to lunch, and I went back to my search. It didn't take much longer. I was still drawing blanks. I spent a few minutes putting the mess back the way I'd found it. Done, enough, and almost nothing to show for it. The sky outside was getting darker and darker. I knew I'd have to leave soon if I wanted to reach my car before the downpour came.

There was a phone on the corner of Emily's desk. I pulled it toward me and began dialing Hump's number. About halfway through, I stopped and hung up. I wrote down the number from the dial and, just to be sure, I flipped through the Metropolitan Atlanta phone book. In the Campbell listings I found an "E. Campbell" with the dorm address and the correct phone number.

One last look around the room, and I fixed the lock and went out into the hall. I pulled the door closed and it held. On the way down the hall, I startled a thin blonde girl in a slip and shower shoes. She didn't scream, but she did the next best thing. She took a flying leap through the nearest open door.

I guess I'd forgotten to yell there was a man on the hall.

CHAPTER FIVE

Hump was in the kitchen when I got to his apartment. He was having a lunch of Kentucky Fried Chicken and beer. I got a beer and sat down across from him. I snaked a leg from the bucket and chewed on it while I told him I'd spent my morning. Near the end of the account, I remembered the tinfoil wad and got it out of my coat pocket. I tossed it to him "I couldn't leave it there for the aunt to find."

"Not much here," Hump said.

"About a quarter-ounce and a chip of hash."

He wiped his hands on a dish towel and stood up. "This chick I know screws like a madwoman with a bit of this in her." He pulled out a drawer and lifted the plastic silver tray. He dropped the tinfoil wad under the tray and replaced it. "Now you know all my secrets."

When he was seated again, I showed him the number I'd copied from the dial in Emily Campbell's dorm room. He finished off the last of the chicken. "This trim I used to do works at Southern Bell. She's one of the blacks who sits by the door so you can't miss her." He belched and threw the last bone in the bucket. "Our problem is that the calls we're interested in might not show up yet. I don't know how the billing system works."

I said I was especially interested in any calls she'd made from the dorm room number on the night I'd been tailing her. If there were any long-distance calls, that might tell us where to look. If there weren't any long-distance calls, we could assume that Eddie is in town. Whoever Eddie is."

After Hump left for the scouting trip at Southern Bell, I had a second beer and tried to decide upon the next step. The phone number check might turn out to be a blind end. If it was, I'd have to find another way of finding Eddie. Maybe The Man would know something. The problem was that I didn't have his phone number. That way my fault. I'd had my ass in the air the whole time at his apartment, and after my to-do with Ferd, I'd stalked out because it made such a good scene.

No help for it. I drove over to The Man's place. I parked next to the black Ford that Ferd had been driving the day before. I went around to the back of the building and beat on the door for a couple of minutes before one of the blacks came down and let me in. I was a bit relieved that it wasn't Ferd. I followed him up the stairs.

"The Man's busy. I'm not sure he can see you."

"Ask him."

I waited out on the landing until he returned a few minutes later and waved me inside. The Man was in the kitchen, closing and locking a small attaché case. He handed it to the black, and the black took it into the bedroom. The Man led me to the bar and I mixed myself a thin drink.

"Hardman, you amaze me. You got it figured out already?"

"Not yet. Just some questions."

The Man sat on the sofa and crossed his legs, careful of his creases. "Ask away."

"When's the last time you saw Emily?"

"The day before my boys ran into you."

"You didn't see her that night? Or the next three days?"

He shook his head. "She gave up on me that night she was at the Dew Drop In Cafe."

"You try to reach her?" I asked.

"I never called her," he said. "I didn't want to make trouble for her."

I asked how that would make trouble for her.

His mouth twisted. "Some nigger calls her up at the dorm, and her roommate takes the call. You don't think that'd make trouble?"

"You don't sound..."

"On the phone I do. So I waited. I thought she'd call me the next day, and she didn't. I thought she was a little mad with me, so I gave her another day to cool off. No call that day. And on the third day, she got killed."

"Did she ever mention somebody named Eddie?"

"Is he the one who did it?"

I said I didn't know. It was just a name that had come up a time or two.

"She never talked to me about other men," he said, with hard-lipped pride.

I decided that was enough for the moment. I asked for and got his phone number.

"Unlisted," he said.

I folded the strip of paper and put it in my wallet. "How's Ferd?"

"He's fine for now, but when you're not working for me any longer, you'd better watch yourself."

"He around now?" It might not work, but a few words might patch things up. It was worth trying.

"Out on an errand." The Man said.

"Walking?"

"He took the Ford."

"The Ford's in the lot downstairs."

"It can't be."

When I insisted that it was, he and I went down the stairs together and around the side of the building. The black Ford was still there. "Now, where the shit...?" The Man began.

He leaned against the window on the passenger side and looked inside. "Oh, God..."

Because he seemed frozen, stunned against that door, I walked around the car and opened the one on the driver's side. Then I saw that Ferd was back, all right. He was stuffed down into the floorboards. His head was toward me, and I could see that someone had beaten him on the head and face until the bone was like mush. One look was enough. I slammed the door shut.

The Man met me as I rounded the rear of the car. "You do this?" He was taking short gulps of air, as if trying to keep the sickness away.

"No," I said, "I got over my mad yesterday."

"I hope you're not lying to me, Hardman," he said.

I followed him back around the building, and up the stairs to the apartment.

A few seconds later, the other black man came out of the bedroom with a thick bundle of newspapers under one arm, and went down the stairs three at a time. The Man followed him to the landing and closed the door behind him.

Remembering it suddenly, I said, "My prints are on the door handle."

"The car's coming back. Ferd isn't." He mixed himself a drink and poured a fresh shot in mine. "The car's in my name."

For the next ten minutes, The Man sat on the sofa and made a series of calls from a list he held on his knee. I didn't learn much about the operation from the few words that got spoken. The Man would ask if Ferd had been by. Then he'd ask if the count was right. Each time, the same two questions. When he finished, he folded the list and put it in his pocket. "It wasn't robbery—or if it was, they didn't get anything."

"What was Ferd doing?"

"Dropping off some goods. He made all the stops."

"When was his last stop?" I asked.

"A bit after one."

I looked at my watch. It was two-twenty-five.

Before I could ask the next question, he answered it for me. "After the drops, Ferd would stop off to see a girl or have a bit of lunch. I didn't expect him back until two-thirty or three o'clock."

"You could have your boys ask around, and see if anybody saw Ferd or the car between one and two."

"I'll do that," The Man said.

"Especially around this area. Somebody picked him up somewhere else, killed him, and then stuffed him in the car and drove the car right over to your parking lot. All in broad daylight. That's a lot of risk for nothing. If it was for nothing."

"You think somebody is trying to tell me something?" The Man asked.

"That's one possibility."

"Why?"

"Maybe somebody wants your paper route," I said.

The Man made a phone call. Ferd's replacement arrived within a quarter-hour. He was short and as broad as a door. He carried a canvas sheath, the kind that hunting rifles are carried in to protect them from bad weather and dirt. But when he pulled the sheath away, I saw that he'd brought a pump shotgun. He put a chair against the bar, facing the door, and sat down with the pump gun across his knees.

I mixed another drink and waited. Before I left, I wanted to be certain that Ferd had been moved without a hitch. During that time, I kept trying to find a connection between the murders of Emily Campbell and Ferd. Emily was having an affair with The Man and Ferd worked for him. That was all. But there had to be more. There was some link I could not see, and that meant I wasn't looking at it from the right angle. Looking at a crime was sometimes like walking around a piece of sculpture at a gallery. From every angle, it was a different piece of sculpture. So it was with a crime. You had to be standing in the right way, with your head in the right place, and then you understood the crime.

So far, I could look at what we had from two angles. One: the death of Emily and Ferd were part of some war in which The Man and his racket had become involved. Kill his girl and kill his helper. Two: the death of the girl was only connected with The Man at a tangent, but there was enough anger and hatred so that it ran over and touched the Man and through him, Ferd. That is, the death of Emily was the real objective. Ferd was almost like an afterthought.

Or, just for the hell of it, how was this for number three? There were usually around 260 or 270 violent deaths a year in Atlanta, shootings and knifings. Perhaps the murders of Emily and Ferd weren't related at all, but just Atlanta keeping the average up for the year.

The black who'd gone to dispose of Ferd's body returned a minute or so after four. (I'd heard The Man refer to him as Horace.) He walked into the eye of the pump gun. That surprised him, but he handled it well. He handed The Man a brown paper sack. I followed The Man into the kitchen, and watched as he dumped the contents onto the kitchen table. One object, wrapped in a piece of newspaper, hit the table with a heavy thump. There was also a wallet, a watch, cuff links and some small change. The Man pushed these aside and unwrapped the heavy object. He pushed it toward me, and I could see that it was a slapjack. It looked like my slapjack.

"Mine," I said. "Ferd took it from me outside the Dew Drop In."

Horace backed me up. Ferd had taken a liking to the slapjack and had started carrying it around in his topcoat pocket. In fact, he'd seen Ferd playing around with it earlier in the day, before he left on his run.

I took the slapjack into the bathroom and ran some water on it until the water dissolved the blood and the paper came free. I tore the bloody paper into small pieces and flushed it down the john. Then I washed the slapjack as well as I could and rolled it in a wad of toilet paper. Back in the living room, I dropped it into my topcoat pocket and left. As soon as I reached my house, I got out an old can of saddle soap and worked over the slapjack until it was clean. Then I put it in an out-of-sight corner of the closet to dry out.

I called Hump a couple of times and finally reached him at five-fifteen. He said the Southern Bell trim had a list of calls made from Emily's dorm room. He expected her in a minute or two. "If you'll come by in an hour, we'll go over them with her."

"Why an hour?"

"Got to pay my dues with her," he said.

I wasted part of the hour with a call to Art Maloney, at his home number. He said there wasn't anything new. To save myself some legwork, I asked if they'd run into anybody named Eddie who was tied to Emily in any way. He perked up and wanted details. I told him that all I knew was that the name had cropped up a couple of times. He might be an ex-boyfriend. Art said he'd have that checked out. And then, surprisingly, he thanked me for the tip. That had to mean that the police were drawing blanks all the way, and were willing to follow up any kind of lead, no matter how vague it was.

Being thanked by a policeman always made my day.

Before I left for Hump's apartment I got the .38 Police Positive out of hiding and put it in my topcoat. I didn't like the way people who had connections with The Man were dropping by the wayside. I didn't want to be the third on that list. Or even the fourth or fifth.

※　※　※

Hump and the Southern Bell trim were in the living room having a drink when I let myself in after knocking. The Southern Bell trim was not really very trim: she weighed about two hundred pounds. In fact, she looked like a busted bale of hay. Her name was Emma Jane Green.

"This sweet young lady did us a lot of good," Hump said.

"It wasn't anything," Emma Jane said. "But don't tell anyone I gave you the numbers."

I said we wouldn't. It was private business.

Hump handed me the penciled list of numbers and destinations. The calls included the tenth of December, the day I'd followed Emily Campbell to the Dew Drop In. "They don't go as far as we'd like," Hump said.

"It might be enough," I said.

"Four of the calls are to the same number in Millhouse," Hump said.

Emma Jane corrected him. "Three are, but the fourth is a collect call from Millhouse."

"From the same number," I said. There was also a call to Athens, Georgia, and one to Spartenburg, South Carolina. I decided to ignore these two for the moment and concentrate on the Millhouse calls. Three of the Millhouse calls were dated the tenth. Two of the calls looked like some kind of bare-minimum charge, as if the call had been completed but the party hadn't been in, or the conversation had been rather short. The final call on the twelfth had run up a tab of $4.25.

"Any way of knowing who these calls were made to?"

"I didn't have time," Emma Jane said.

When Emma Jane got ready to leave, I looked at Hump to see if I should put out some money. He read my mind and shook his head. After a bit of small-talk, Hump walked her downstairs to her car. As soon as the door closed behind them, I direct-dialed the number in Millhouse. The phone rang five times before it was answered.

"Hello." It was a surly, go-to-hell greeting.

"I want to speak to Ed."

"Ed who?"

"Isn't this the fire station?" I asked.

"You kidding?" He laughed. "That's a good one."

"This isn't the fire station?" I insisted.

"It's Ben Sharp's Pool Hall."

I said I was sorry and hung up. Hump came in, puffing from the climb up the stairs. I looked at him and then at the closed bedroom door. He grinned. "That girl's been eating boxes of cornstarch."

"But she seems to have a good heart," I said.

"And good moral character," Hump said. Then he dismissed it. "You try the number yet?"

"Ben Sharp's Pool Hall."

"We going to play some pool?" Hump asked.

"Looks like it."

I had a small drink while he showered. While he dressed I stood in the doorway and told him about the death of Ferd, and that it had been done with my slapjack. Hump stopped in midstride at that, dug down into the bottom of the clothes closet, and brought out a battered gym bag. He unzipped it and took out a rolled-up sweat suit. Inside, there was the .38 I'd given him a year-and-a-half before, one I'd taken off a drunk one night.

"I don't like the way this one is heading," he said. He put on a knee-length black leather coat and dropped the gun in his pocket. "There's blood in the soup already."

We arrived in Millhouse at eight o'clock, give or take a minute or two.

CHAPTER SIX

The main tourist attraction in Millhouse is a slave auction block in the center of a little park beside the courthouse. One corner of the block was chipped and blackened in a midnight explosion during the civil rights demonstrations, back in 1964. Other than that, it's a town of forty thousand that locks up tight at seven every night, except for the two movie houses and two or three hamburger and beer joints.

Hump pulled into an all-night truck stop on the edge of town. While the car was being gassed, I walked back to talk to the attendant and asked directions to the pool hall. He gave them with the ease of someone often asked. He repeated them once more to be sure I had them and, with a look toward the front of the car, where Hump was, he lowered his voice a notch or two. "He won't be welcome."

"Him?" I laughed. "He's my driver."

We followed the directions. Through the main part of town, one mile past the city-limits sign, left at the first fork, a right on a dirt road just past a combination grocery store and gas station. Half a mile down that road and you couldn't miss it.

"From what the gas-pumper said back there," I said, "you're not going to be much welcome."

"That's your problem," Hump said. "You owe me for the Dew Drop In visit the other might."

"*That* silly promise," I said, and Hump laughed at me.

It was there, just like the station attendant said, a low, flat building constructed from cinderblocks. There was a narrow door near the left corner and a single window to balance the door on the right. A Coca-Cola sign above the door was flaked around the edges and pocked from what was probably some late-hour target shooting.

The packed-dirt parking lot could have held a hundred or so cars, but there were only a dozen or so there when we drove up, all of them clustered together in the darkness around the right side of the building. Hump avoided them and parked on the left side, nearer the front door. I guess I could have gone in without Hump and asked my questions. But my dealings with rednecks in the past had convinced me that they didn't like strangers asking questions. That could lead to trouble and, if there was going to be trouble, I wanted Hump's two hundred and seventy pounds of bad-ass on my side. Hump didn't like the redneck shit, but he'd spent a lot of time around other parts of the country where the black-hate pushed at him in subtle ways. I believed, without ever talking to him about it, that he preferred it in the open, where he could deal with it in the physically violent way that got respect if not understanding.

I went in first and Hump ducked in after me. The aisle between the pool tables was wide enough for us to walk side by side, and Hump moved up level with me. The pool tables covered about two-thirds of the area of the long room. To the right there was a beer bar, and to the end near the front of the building, a wired-in cage where the business of the table rentals was handled.

We headed for the bar. As soon as a few of the pool shooters saw us, there was a muttered "nigger" or two, loud enough for us to hear but not loud enough to appear to be a challenge. I sat at the curved end of the bar, near the wired-in cage. Hump remained standing, on my left, between me and the length of the bar, where two young rednecks in jeans and denim jackets sat talking to the bartender. The bartender, a thin crew-cut man in a dirty half-apron, ignored us for two or three minutes. Then, wiping the bar top with a rag as he came, he edged toward us. "Yeah?"

"Two beers."

"We're out of beer."

"One beer then," I said.

The bartender grinned. The gap-toothed pleasure meant he'd won, had put it over on the nigger and the nigger-lover. He went over to the Coca-Cola box and got out three bottles of Bud. He opened two of them and placed them in front of the denim-jacketed young rednecks. Slowly, as if the cap didn't want to come off, he opened the third one and brought it down to me. He placed it on the counter in front of me, along with a paper cup. I dropped a dollar bill on the counter and watched while he made change from his pocket. He remained there, watching me. I lifted the beer and handed it to Hump.

"He's the thirsty one," I said.

Hump took the bottle from my hand and, in one fluid motion, lifted it to his mouth. He didn't bring it down until it was empty. He put the bottle on the bar top with a loud thump.

"Hey!" The shout was from one of the young rednecks down the bar. It sounded more like surprise than anger, but Hump and I turned to face him as he left his bar stool and walked toward us. He had carrot-red hair, a mass of pimples across the bridge of his nose, and brown acne scars on his cheekbones. Next to me I heard the gritty slip of Hump's shoes on the concrete floor as he set his feet.

"I might be wrong … but aren't you Hump Evans?"

"You're not wrong," Hump said.

The redhead put out his hand. "God, the times I've seen you on TV."

Hump gave the hand a hard squeeze. "This is my friend, Mr. Hardman."

"Glad to meet you." But he wasn't really looking at me. He motioned down the bar. "I want you to meet my friend, Benny. Benny, come down here and meet Hump Evans."

The boy came, but he came slowly, as if this friendly reaction to a black wasn't the usual social thing to do in Millhouse. He didn't offer to shake hands, but there was some of the same awe in his face that I saw in the redhead's.

I took that moment to see how this registered with the bartender. "Two more beers."

He stuck to his story. "I'm out of beer."

"Two beers, Mason," the redhead said. "If they can't buy them, I will."

"Your daddy…"

"My daddy ain't here." The redhead sounded hard and mean. I'd seen that before: around Hump, the fans all seemed to grow hair on their chests.

"He ain't going to like it," the bartender said, but he went for the beers.

"I'm Marshall Sharp. My daddy owns the place."

"It's a nice place," I said. I even looked around and nodded a couple of times. When the beers came I tried to pay, but Marshall waved my money away and said they were on him. The bartender didn't like that, either, but he clamped his mouth shut and moved to the far end of the bar. The kids spent the next few minutes asking Hump about other pro players he knew. Hump put on a friendly attitude that I knew he didn't feel, and the talk went on and on while I tried to think of a way to move the subject matter around to Eddie, whoever he was, and the phone calls.

Sometime later, during a break in the feverish fan talk, Marshall asked what we were doing in Millhouse.

"Passing through," Hump said.

"We got lost," I said.

Marshall laughed. "This far off the main highway, you'd have to be."

I decided to try a story out on the kid. "We're just kidding. We met a girl at a party a couple of nights ago. When she found out we'd be passing through Millhouse, she asked us to stop off and give a message to a guy who hangs out in here."

"What's his name?"

"Eddie."

"Eddie Spence?" He checked himself. He was suspicious now. He'd made a slip, and he didn't like it.

I turned to Hump. "Was the last name Spence?"

"You asking me?" Hump took a pull at the bottle. "You were the one doing all the talking to her."

"But I was smashed, and you know I never remember names the next day."

"You mean we came all this way out of the way ...?" Hump let it die out. He tapped Marshall on the shoulder. "If that's not a fuck-up, I've never seen one."

I waited for Hump's booming laugh to fade. "All I remember is Eddie."

"He'd be a young guy," Hump said.

"Eddie Spence is young," Marshall said.

"The girl said she called him here all the time," I said.

The other kid, Benny, decided to chip in. "That would be Spence. She used to call him now and then. I remember one night, she called him two or three times. I know, because I answered the phone."

Marshall was trying to get his attention. To warn him, I thought. "Has he been in tonight?" I asked quickly.

"He hasn't been in for three or four days," Benny said.

"I think he's been sick," Marshall said.

Of the two, I believed Benny. I wasn't sure about Marshall. "Too bad," I said. "The message was kind of important."

"You can leave it with me," Marshall said.

"Eddie only, that's what the girl said."

"You a cop?"

Hump and I gave him our best surprised looks. Then we laughed until the back of my throat hurt. "Him?" Hump sputtered, "Him?"

I got out my wallet and handed him a card I'd had printed especially for such occasions. It had my name on it and a phony address and phone number. It said I was an agent for Nationwide. "Not a chance," I said, while he read the card.

"Why you worrying about a cop, Marshall?" Hump asked. "Has Eddie been in trouble?"

That was one of the benefits of using Hump. Marshall still wanted to trust him. "Yeah, a time or two, but nothing really serious."

Benny blurted out "You call shooting at a guy at a drive-in ... ?"

The way his face contorted, I was sure that Marshall had stepped on his foot. He choked and swallowed the rest of it. He didn't like Marshall any better for it, but he'd gotten the message.

Hump saw that we were overstaying our welcome. He changed the subject and told a long, colorful story about one night when he and three other pro players had gone to a bar in Dallas. It was a fairly funny story that I'd heard once or twice before. It sounded like the main fight in a John Wayne movie.

Then, with Marshall and Benny laughing away, we finished our beers, said goodnight and got the hell out of there.

On the way back through town, I had Hump stop at one of the hamburger and beer joints. Hump was moody after we left the pool hall. I think it was because he didn't like the kind of double-standard that the redneck kid practiced. And maybe, though I wasn't sure of this, he might have been a little pissed at me for putting him in that situation.

I ordered four burgers to go and a six-pack of Bud. While the burgers were cooking, I went to the pay phone and looked up the Spences in the phone book. There were five listed. I got some dimes from the counterman and started with the first one. On the third call, I had the right one.

"I'd like to speak to Eddie."

"He's not here," the woman said.

"I need to get in touch with him," I said, "and it's important."

"He's in Atlanta."

"Where can I reach him in Atlanta?"

"Who are you?" the woman asked. "Do I know you?"

I gave her a phony name and said I was from Nationwide.

"We don't want any," the woman said, and hung up.

I wrote down the phone number and the address. The burgers and the beer were packaged and ready. I paid for them and carried them out to the car. On the drive back to Atlanta, we took turns driving while the other one ate. I'd considered a visit to the Spence house, but Hump had argued against it. "He's been in trouble before, and she's probably had practice lying for him." I'd given up on it then and decided to put it up to Art Maloney when we got back to Atlanta.

Headed toward Hump's apartment, I had him stop at a gas station so I could use the pay phone. I called Art, but he was out. I left my home number and said I could be reached there in twenty minutes or so. Hump pulled up beside my Ford, down the street from his apartment building. Before I got out, I said he might as well call it a day. He said he'd be at home all evening if I needed him. He was going to try the grass and hash out on the girl he thought would like them.

"Don't get too stoned."

"There's no such thing," he said.

I patted the gun in his coat pocket. "And watch yourself."

He said he would, patting my coat pocket, as if to say the same thing to me.

Art didn't return my call. Instead, he drove over to my house and found me reading the blue streak edition of the evening paper,

The Journal. I'd gone all the way through the paper and found no mention of anyone finding Ferd's body. There was always the chance they'd never find it if The Man didn't want it found.

"I was in the area when I heard about your call," Art said.

I poured us each a good shot of J&B and gave him a brief account of the trip to Millhouse. "There's some connection between this Eddie Spence and the Campbell girl. I don't know what it is, but it's there."

"He might be able to tell us something," Art said. He got out his notebook and went into the bedroom, where my phone was. I heard him talking to somebody named Frank for a few minutes, and then he came back. "Frank Ransome," he explained. "Those local policemen jump a bit faster for the G.B.I. than they do for us." He looked at his empty glass. "After the Millhouse police talk to the parents, he'll call me back here"

I put a few ice cubes in his glass and brought the bottle into the living room. "How's the murder business?"

"Funny you should ask." He gave me a tight look. "The call just came in that a couple looking for necking space found the body of a naked black male, no identification, head popped open like a watermelon."

"Nobody I know," I said. "Where'd they find him?"

"In the woods over near that new Executive Suite apartment complex." He sipped the scotch. "We're checking his prints now."

"Atlanta's unsolved murder for the day," I said.

"That's likely."

Forty minutes later, the man from the G.B.I. called back. I followed Art into the bedroom and watched over his shoulder as he wrote down *Clearview Hotel, off Houston.* I left him talking to Ransome and got my topcoat from the closet, careful so that he didn't see the weight of the gun, and put it on.

Out in the driveway, Art stopped beside the door of his unmarked car. "You planning on coming along?"

"If it's all right. I'm queer for cop work."

He nodded, and I went around the car and got into the passenger seat. "The Millhouse police called from the Spence house. Ransome told them to stay there until we call back. That's so they can't try to warn Eddie Spence … if they haven't already." That was aimed at me for the phone call I'd made in Millhouse.

"He might be armed," I said, remembering what the kid, Benny, had said about Eddie Spence shooting at somebody at a drive-in.

Art called in and asked that a patrol car meet us at the Clearview.

The entrance to the Clearview Hotel is just a narrow doorway leading into a stairwell. There's an old neon sign over the doorway, but it's broken and doesn't light up. I'd been in the place once before, a couple of years earlier, when I'd been looking for a wino who'd cut up another one over a pint of muscatel. It was a rat's nest for the one- or two-day trade, the drifters.

Before we went up, Art sent the two uniformed cops from the patrol car around the block, to cover the rear exit and the fire escape. He gave them a couple of minutes by his watch to get into position, and then we went up the stairs. The night clerk, a fat, oily man in a dirty blue sport shirt, stood up when he heard us crossing the lobby. He pushed a registration card and a ballpoint pen at us. From the nasty smile, I guessed that he thought we were a couple of queers looking for a door we could lock. Art flipped open his wallet and showed his I.D. The clerk took his time reading it.

"Eddie Spence," Art said.

"Spence." The clerk reached under the counter and brought up his metal box of file cards. He slowly worked his way back to the "S" divider. When he found the right card he kept a finger in the space and lifted out the card. He held it out to Art.

"312," Art said. "Is he in?"

The clerk turned and looked at the pegboard where the keys were hanging. "He's here. His key's not here."

I leaned past Art. "He have any calls tonight?"

"Not tonight," the clerk said.

Art looked at the battered switchboard behind the desk. "No call *now* either," he said.

The clerk nodded.

"Does the room face the street or the back?"

"The street."

Art and I started up the stairs at a run. When we reached the landing and saw the "3" on the door, Art unbuttoned his top-coat and suit jacket. Just at that moment, we heard a door slam in the distance. We hit the hall at a run, going in the direction of the slamming sound. I hesitated at the open doorway about halfway down the hall on the left, just long enough to see the "312" painted there and to be sure that the room was empty. Then I sprinted after Art. I reached the fire-escape door just a step behind him. As Art's hands touched the push bar, we heard the shots. The shots were very close together, but it sounded like three or four.

The light was out at the top of the fire escape. We had to go down a step at a time, a lot slower than we wanted to. When we reached the dark alleyway, we could hear footsteps running toward us but nothing running away from us. A few feet from the bottom of the fire escape, we found the dark shape slumped and tilted against the wall. The running steps toward us slowed and faltered as a flashlight swept across us and then down at the shape at our feet. It was one of the uniformed policeman. Art squatted beside him in the wavering light. Past Art's shoulder, I could see that the cop had been hit in the neck and the chest. His gun was still in his holster.

Art straightened up. "He's dead." He pounded the butt of his pistol against the brick wall, and a thin powder of brick dust showered down upon the dead man. We left the dead cop with his buddy, and went down the alley to the street. We circled the block, looking, but we didn't know what Spence looked like. We had to give it up. Art placed a call from his car and we went back down the alley.

It was cold in the dark there. The wind swirled around in its tight confinement. The cop we'd left there was still on guard over his buddy, but he'd turned off his flashlight, as if he'd seen more than he wanted to. I offered him a cigarette and, in the windy flare of my lighter, I saw that he was still in shock.

I patted him on the shoulder, and Art and I went up the fire escape to room 312, to see what the junk in the room could tell us about Eddie Spence.

Art went to the window first. There was an ashtray on the ledge and the single chair was nearby. I moved around Art and looked down into the street. I could see Art's unmarked car and the patrol car. Eddie Spence had been at the window. He'd seen us, and that was how he'd gotten the jump on us.

Leaving the window, Art pulled an open suitcase from under the bed. He poked around in it with his pen, not because he was afraid of disturbing anything important, but because it seemed to contain mainly dirty underwear. I left him at that and went into the bathroom. There was nothing in there except for shaving gear and a damp towel.

Behind me, Art said, "Look at this, Jim."

I returned from the bathroom and did a knee bend beside him. He'd worked the dirty clothes around until he'd uncovered a framed photo. It was a shot of a young boy and girl standing in front of a swimming pool. The girl was in a brief two-piece suit. The boy was wearing a cut-off pair of jeans. He had a crew cut and the heavily-muscled torso of an athlete. I leaned closer and looked at the girl. She'd been three or four years younger then, but it looked like Emily Campbell, the girl I'd seen twice, once in the dorm parking lot and again in the Dew Drop In Cafe.

"I think it's Emily Campbell," I said.

"And I'd give odds the boy is Eddie Spence."

"No bet," I said.

When the rest of the police crew showed up, Art and I went back down to the lobby. The clerk was upset, and he was more cooperative now. From the back of the card, he gave us the information that Eddie Spence had checked into the hotel on the 11th, the day after I'd tailed Emily Campbell and two days before she was murdered.

That, and the death of the young cop downstairs, made him dog meat as far as Art was concerned.

CHAPTER SEVEN

The background bits and pieces came in on Eddie Spence all through the morning hours. Art didn't leave his office while the manhunt got mounted, and he was still there when I dropped by at nine a.m. after a few hours sleep. He was red-eyed, and cigarettes had soured his tongue, and he walked like he had a hundred-pound pack on his back. I brought him a pint of coffee and he looked at it like he might throw up. But for all that, he'd pieced together a pretty good background on Eddie Spence. I sat down across from him, lit my first cigarette of the day, and listened to it.

Up until a year ago, the Spences had lived in Mason, Georgia, the small farming town where Arch Campbell and his family were the rich and powerful planters and landowners. Eddie Spence and Emily Campbell were in the same class in high school, and they'd gone together until late in the first semester of their senior year, when Arch Campbell had somehow contrived to put pressure on the Spence family. That pressure had probably been economic, and the end result had been the breakup of the romance between Emily and Eddie. Eddie Spence was an all-state halfback with scholarship offers from the big schools up and down the Eastern Seaboard, and he'd been leaning toward Dooley and Georgia until the breakup. Not long after that he'd disappeared from Mason, and the next time his family heard from him he was in boot camp in San Diego. From San Diego, after boot camp, he came East again, to aviation electrician school at Jacksonville. At the end of the twenty weeks, he ranked high enough in his class to be allowed to pick the billet he wanted, a VU squadron based at the Naval Air Station at Jacksonville. His work with the squadron had been excellent, and he'd been in no trouble until the spring before, when he'd gone AWOL. A routine check of liberty cards and leave papers in the Jacksonville bus station had sent him back to the base for a Captain's Mast and a sentence of restriction to base and extra duty. As soon as he was free to leave the base, on his first liberty, he took off again. This time he reached Atlanta, and was there for a whole day before he was caught.

"That must have been the day he called Emily at her dorm and her roommate took the call," I said.

"We don't know whether he saw her that time or not."

I said I was fairly certain that he hadn't.

This time when Eddie was returned to Jacksonville there'd been a court-martial, and he'd been given an undesirable discharge. He joined his family at Mason and told them a story about receiving a medical discharge because of an old football injury. Not long after that, the Spence family moved from Mason to Millhouse. Eddie had taken night courses to finish high school and had worked as a mechanic at one of the body shops in town but, according to his family, he kept talking about moving to Atlanta and went there several times to look for a job. Then, two days before the death of Emily Campbell, he'd packed a suitcase and moved to Atlanta. He checked into the Clearview Hotel and paid a week in advance. In his five days in the hotel, the clerks said, he'd seldom gone out. Just for breakfast, lunch and supper.

"I doubt that," Art said. "You keep the key, go out the back way, and the clerks would swear you were still in."

The night clerk remembered that Eddie Spence had gone out for supper the night the girl had been murdered and had been back by seven. He hadn't gone out again that night.

"But he admits he didn't see Eddie again that night," Art said. "All he knows is that Spence didn't pass through the lobby again that night."

"Hard to prove," I said.

Art shook his head. That meant, I thought, that he wasn't sure that Eddie would ever get to trial. The slip between the cup and the lip was to be a cop bullet or two. I'd seen it happen once that way. The pimp who'd shot old Johnny Freeman, one of the department favorites, had been standing with his hands coming up empty when Ben Evert shot him twice. Then Ben had jammed a "clean" gun in the waistband of the pimp's trousers, and that was that. Shot while resisting arrest.

"We're looking at him for a couple of other jobs, too," Art said.

That was the police mind at work. Eddie Spence had a gun and he'd used it, and that meant he was a "possible" for every crime committed in the area since he'd moved to town. There was a cabbie murder-robbery in Sandy Springs, the shooting of a service station attendant in Northeast Atlanta, and the holdup of a fried chicken hut out on Ponce De Leon. It would clean up a lot of paperwork if he measured up for one or all of those. The only crime that they didn't have him tabbed as a "possible" for was the murder of "that spade" who'd been found out near the new housing development. That was Ferd, and there just wasn't any way I could let Art know there was a chance that Eddie Spence might really have had a hand in that one.

I was getting ready to leave, when a man from the photo lab brought in a stack of prints and put them on Art's desk. They were dupes they'd made from a recent photo of Eddie Spence that the Millhouse Police had found somewhere. I pocketed twenty or so. I got as far as the door before Art stopped me.

"You keep acting like you're a private investigator without being one, and you're going to get into trouble."

I gave him my best go-to-hell grin. "Nothing in the law that says I can't ask a few questions, or a do a favor or two for a friend."

"On that fire escape last night, I thought I saw you carrying a shooter."

"Made out of soap," I said, "just like the one that John D. used in his jailbreak."

"I'd like to see it," Art said.

"Sorry. I showered with it and it all went down the drain, but I'll carve you another one."

"Just don't let me find you with a gun," Art said.

"You won't find me."

Once I was out on the street, I found a pay phone and called the number The Man had given me.

The Man looked up from the photo of Eddie Spence. "So this is the one?"

I said it seemed that way at the moment. "He and Emily had a thing back in high school. Maybe he never gave up on it and didn't like it when she did."

"And Ferd?"

I shook my head. "That's the hard one, unless he'd been watching Emily and saw Ferd with her."

"It's possible," The Man said. "He picked her up a few times for me . . . not out at Tech, but from some places around town."

"That might be it. He's from redneck country. Maybe he thought Ferd was a boyfriend."

"That would take some imagination."

"He might just have one." I got up from the sofa and crossed in front of the guard with the pump gun. His eyes were closed, but his finger was curled around the outside of the trigger guard. "But he's got trouble. He killed a cop, and the holes are going to close up. If he had any sense, he'd get the hell out of town and head for the boondocks. The only thing is that he might be too crazy-mad to do that."

The Man lit one of his special-blend cigarettes. I watched the hand with the lighter, and there wasn't a tremor.

"If he's still in town," I went on, "then he's got a reason to be here."

"What reason?"

"If he knows about you, then you're probably his reason."

"You're saying I'm the target?"

"Or I am."

"Why you?" The Man asked.

"If he's watching this place, he's seen me coming and going. And last night, at the hotel, he got away because he was watching the street. I think he knows what I look like, and he might want some of my hide for bringing the trouble down on him."

"You can move in with me, Hardman." There was a wry curl to his lip.

"I've still got some moving around to do." I got out a scrap of paper and wrote down Hump's phone number and his address. "You can reach me here."

He raised his eyebrows in a question.

"Hump Evans' place."

"What do you want me to do?"

"Pass the photos around. Anybody sees him, calls you."

"If anybody sees him," The Man said, "he's blood meat."

"No. You call me, and I'll get a few carloads of cops with riot guns, and we'll get him."

"I want him dead."

I let that hang in the air for a moment or two. "The cops just might want him dead, too."

He understood that.

"He's got a shooter, and he's good with it. You try to take him by yourself, and it's going to be a bloody mess. You'll lose a couple of people, and the cops'll end up there anyway."

"They call me, and I call you."

"Right."

He nodded. "Done."

❧ ❧ ❧

"I miss all the fun." Hump was padding around the kitchen in his big, wide bare feet. He was frying up half a dozen eggs and half a pound of bacon. That was his breakfast. I'd already eaten.

I opened the paper bag and got out a couple of changes of underwear and socks and three new shirts. I'd picked them up downtown at Davidson's. "You might not miss the next fun. Your uncle has come to visit for a few days."

"Why has my uncle come to visit?"

"He's too scared shitless to go home," I said.

"And you think this Eddie might come visiting, too?"

"Yes."

"Watch my eggs."

Hump went into the bedroom and I could hear him rooting around in some junk, probably in the closet. I scooped the eggs onto a plate and put them on the table. Hump came out of the bedroom a few seconds later with an ornately-worked double-barreled shotgun. He'd broken it open and was thumbing shells into it.

"Had a Day for me the year after I got hurt. Hump Evans Day. Got given some silly things, but the silliest was this Austrian hunting gun. Liked to laughed my ass off when they gave it to me." The shotgun loaded and closed, he leaned it against the living room wall, behind the easy chair. "Be my guest, if you happen to get to it before me."

He sat down at the table across from me and began eating. Between mouthfuls, he said, "Never fired it but once … went out in the wood one morning … gave a tree both barrels from about ten feet … damned near blew that tree down … damned near tore my shoulder off."

I got the coffee pot and filled our cups. "How was last night?"

"That Campbell girl had good taste in grass."

"And the girl?" I asked.

"She's my friend forever."

"Is that why they call you Hump?"

He grinned. "That came later. My first year in the pros, we had this defensive end coach. When we'd do wind sprints, he'd yell, 'Hump it! Hump it!' and one day I got so wore down, I said I just couldn't hump anymore."

"And the name stuck?"

"Like the fat girl you always get introduced to at a party."

I spent the afternoon on the sofa snoozing, while Hump watched the soap operas. I got up around five and showered. I put in a call to Art's home number but his wife, Edna, said he was still asleep after the double shift. I gave her Hump's number, and she said she'd have him call when he got up.

Art didn't call until around seven. "You got anything, Jim?"

"I ran out of miracles."

"You change your phone number?"

"I'm at Hump's, in hiding."

A pause. "From what?"

"I'm not sure. Maybe some crazy with a gun."

"With the whole force after him, he hasn't got time to worry about you," Art said.

"Wish I could believe that."

"If he's in Atlanta, he's dug himself a deep hole."

"He might be in Millhouse," I said.

"Not as far as we can tell. We've got the Spence house staked out, and we're watching the pool hall, too."

"Bet the redneck pool sharks like that."

"They don't know about it," Art said. "G.B.I. put a couple of working-stiff types in there, drinking beer and shooting eight-ball." He paused. "Before I forget about it, it seems there's some hard feeling about a white man who brought a spade in there last night."

"Just my bit for civil rights," I said.

"That's the way they see it, too."

"Tough titty."

Art laughed and hung up.

Around ten, while we were watching the Bulls gut the Hawks on the tube, Art called back. "Just got word from a patrol car. They think they saw Spence, or somebody damned near like him. They lost him on Trinity Avenue. We're flooding the area."

When Art hung up, I dialed The Man's number. Trinity Avenue was only a few blocks from his place. It could mean that Eddie was headed in his direction. On the third ring, The Man answered. He heard me out and thanked me.

"If this shit doesn't ease off," he said, "I'm thinking about a long trip to Europe."

"Raise my pay and I'll go with you."

He laughed and the line went dead.

A bit after midnight Art called and said they'd given up the search around Trinity Avenue. If the man seen there had really been Eddie Spence, then he'd dropped out of sight again.

Around one, we gave up on the Randolph Scott movie and called it a night. I slept on the sofa, with the Police Positive on the floor nearby in reaching distance. During the night I dreamed, and the odd part is that I remembered the dream afterwards. Usually I don't. I guess it was a deal I made with myself years ago, that I wouldn't remember the dreams. And now, some twenty years later, I'd forgotten why I'd ever decided to block the memory of the dreams. I guess it's just habit now.

It was too real, that dream. It was about betrayal, and it was a long time before I understood why. It was about a young boy and a young girl, and the final day of a summer, when the love went sour. I was that young boy, and the girl was Maryann, and it was late August of the year we graduated from high school. A summer spent at the lake or the tennis court. And the last day. The week before she was to leave for Agnes Scott. For me, there wasn't anything ahead. A job, or maybe the service. No money for college. That day: seated on a bench in the fenced-in tennis court at the city park. Waiting. Cool shadows pacing across the court, so that it would soon be completely in shadows. Clocks and the shadow-time telling me that she was late. Then, when I'd just about given up on her, the little brother riding his bike down the dirt path around the court toward me. Note in hand. Not liking me and glad that he could deliver the note. A note from Maryann's mother that said Maryann had left a week early so that she could visit an aunt in Little Rock. Regrets for not having reached me earlier. The dream ending with the little brother riding his bike away, like the final crane shot in some goddamn movie.

And waking on Hump's sofa, I wondered how dreams used to be before we had movies to structure our dreams out of single shots, and out of camera movement.

And before I went to sleep again, I asked myself why I'd had that particular dream, and what the hell it meant, anyway.

And then I knew. There was Eddie Spence and Emily Campbell, and maybe what had happened to them some two or three years ago. Maybe that triggered the dream. The betrayal that's behind a lot of dreams.

CHAPTER EIGHT

1951. Maryann and that young love gone to Little Rock, and on to Agnes Scott. Me with a house painter for a father, and she with all the money. It wasn't really big money, just big in that little town. And all the sick pretensions that went with it. That summer, I sat in her house one night while she got ready for Agnes Scott. A sewing kit on her knees, she was changing the labels in the clothing she was taking with her. Labels from her mother's dresses and coats, sewn in so that when she got to college, they'd be seen and appreciated.

Maryann off to Little Rock and Agnes Scott, while I caught the bus to Fort Jackson. Drafted. Maybe we reached our destinations about the same time. Tea parties or the rifle range. Dorm life or hand-to-hand combat. And then, when basic training was over, I was off to Japan to a Military Police company.

And a couple of months later, I killed my first man.

It was an early morning raid on a bar owned by three master-sergeants. The word was that the bar was dealing in the black market and paying for the goods in American Military currency. It was the dealing in the currency that bothered the Army. It was against regulations to take the military currency off the base. You were paid in it and you could use it on the base, but you were supposed to convert it to yen for use off base. From the rumors of the amounts being paid out, it sounded like they had quite a stockpile, and the Army wanted to know where it came from.

My post was at the rear of the bar, in the shadow of a nearby building. It was a snow moon that night, with almost no light

down on the street. On the dot by my watch, I heard the splinter-
ing of the front door and the shouting in Japanese and American
voices. I was relaxed where I was, except for the cold, knowing it
was over, when a window about fifty yards from me, at the rear
of the bar, slid open. A dark shape hurdled out and landed facing
me. I got the service .45 out of my holster.

"Halt!" The man turned and started to run. I charged the
pistol and shouted, "Halt or I'll fire!"

The man only sprinted harder. I got the .45 in line and aimed
for the legs. Just before I fired the man bent forward, as if trying
to make a smaller target. I shouted "Halt!" again and squeezed
off a round. I didn't see him bend, and the .45 slug raked his
back and blew off the back of his head. At least, that's the way we
figured it out later.

It was the only shot fired on the raid. The man I killed was a
forty-year-old Japanese bartender who lived in a room in back of
the bar. It came out later that he had nothing to do with the black
market dealings or the use of the military currency.

I was restricted to post for a week while there was an investigation. At the end of that time I was called into Major Bartlet's
office. The meeting was brief. "Your record's been good. I don't
believe that punishment's called for in the incident at the Half
Moon Bar. Not your fault, really, but I think it's time for your
rotation to other duties."

The next morning, I was on a plane to Seoul.

I was doing gate-guard duty at Fort McPherson when my discharge date came up. In my time there, I'd come to know and like
Atlanta. So I took my discharge there and moved into Atlanta, to
see how long my savings and my mustering-out pay would last.
In a couple of months, I started looking around for something to
do. There was college and the G.I. bill, but I wasn't sure I could

stand the poverty on $110 a month. In the bars around town and the guys I met there, I could see there were chances in the rackets. I was leaning that way, and I could see the offers shaping up. At the last minute I changed my mind and went as far as I could in the other direction. I joined the Atlanta Police Department. For the first few years promotion was slow, and I helped it along by taking night courses at several of the colleges around town.

Art Maloney and I started at the same time, and we moved along at the same rate, taking some of the same night classes and being promoted on the same lists. We were friends, too, pretty close friends. But when the mess came and the reform blow hit the town, I got sucked into the middle of it and he didn't.

It was a woman, of course. It had to be.

Her name was Marcy King, and she said she was an executive secretary at a big company, Marsh and Wheeler. All I knew was that it was an investment company, and that was all I wanted to know. It didn't seem to matter at the time. I didn't think Marcy would be working there much longer, anyway. I was in love, and I couldn't see myself with a working wife. That was when I found that run-down house and put myself in hock to the mortgage company. I didn't tell Marcy about the house. It was to be a surprise. Art was helping me with some repairs and general do-it-yourself, and I thought I'd just about put away enough money for a professional inside and outside paint job.

And then the shit and piss hit the fan. The reform wind was blowing, and it blew the door off Marsh and Wheeler. It wasn't just an investment company. It was a washing machine for racket money. It went into Marsh and Wheeler dirty, and it came out clean, with a profit. And, as a sideline, it functioned as a payoff center for all the guys on the take.

The heads rolled up and down Peachtree Street. And mine was one. Not that they could prove I'd taken any money. They couldn't. And nobody at the hearings said I'd given them protection. But my name dropped in, a time or two. Like television advertising, a lot more implied than stated outright. *Yes, James Hardman was going with one of our secretaries, a Miss King. As far as I know, there was no payoff to Hardman, but then I didn't handle all the payoffs.* And just when I seemed to have weathered the blow, I got called into the Division Chief's office and shown a copy of the statement Marcy had given the Grand Jury investigator. Most of it was about the operation of Marsh and Wheeler. Only one small section concerned me.

> QUESTION: *Do you know a James Hardman of the Atlanta Police Department?*
> ANSWER: *Yes.*
> QUESTION: *Under what circumstances did you know James Hardman?*
> ANSWER: *I was told by Mr. Avery Marsh that I was to cultivate Mr. Hardman.*

I stopped reading there. In fifteen minutes they had my resignation, and in fifteen minutes more I'd cleaned out my desk and walked out the front door.

To spend the time after that doing anything that wasn't too much work, and paid fifty dollars or more a day. In time, Raymond Hutto came along with his propositions, and his dope flights from New York. The first time out I almost got hijacked, and after that I'd worked Hump in as a back-up man. But bringing dope back from New York wasn't a regular job. It got risky if you made too many trips. The stain from a couple of years before marked me as a natural, and I knew the narco squad knew me. It was just a matter of time before I got outguessed.

Marcy King was back in town. I'd heard it here and there. From Art and Edna, from Hump. I don't know where she'd been, only that she hadn't done time. Sometimes, late at night, I wanted to see her, and sometimes I wanted to kick out four or five of her teeth. But in the daylight, I knew I didn't want to do either of those things. All that was past, and just shadow-fighting.

Around six I got up and made a pot of coffee. I got the *Constitution* from out in the hall and read it from cover to cover, while I drank coffee and listened to Hump snoring away in the bedroom, with the snorting and wheezing of a man who's had his nose broken a time or two.

He woke up while I was under the shower. I came back through the bedroom and found his bed empty. He was in the kitchen, drinking milk straight from the half-gallon carton,

"You got anything planned for today?" he asked.

"I thought I'd stay alive."

He grinned at me and started breakfast.

Late in the afternoon, Art called and said that he was going down to Millhouse to talk to Eddie Spence's mother and father. I said I'd be happy and proud to go along.

Art didn't say much at first. The Friday afternoon traffic was thick and reckless, and he seemed preoccupied with the driving, keeping the unmarked cruiser's fenders undented. Then, when the commuter traffic slackened and dropped away and the road was straight and level, he had time for me.

"Who's your client?"

"I'm not a P.I. I don't have a client."

"If you were a P.I.,. I could make you tell me," Art said.

"That's a good reason not to be one."

That burned him some, and I could see the flush on his face that meant he was holding his Irish down. "All right, just between us, not for the record, who're you working for?"

"That's almost as nice as saying please." I kept him waiting while I looked out at the wintering trees and the frosted stubble of the farmland. "How does Hugh Muffin sound to you?"

"Like a lot of clout. Why'd he pick you?"

"I've done him a friendly favor or two in the past," I said.

"No," Art said. "What's his put in on the Campbell case?"

"He's tight friends with the Campbell girl's father."

"Can I check this with him?" Art asked.

"Only if you tell I said you could ask. Otherwise, he might deny it."

"To me," Art said, "that sounds phony."

"Protects himself and me."

"It's got a stink to it."

I lit a smoke and offered him one. "That's the way I make my living now. In a couple of years I've gotten so that I don't even notice any more."

"Marcy's in town."

I didn't say anything. Art had told me before, a time or two, and each time like it was news. Maybe he kept forgetting, but I doubted it. Art and his wife, Edna, had been out with Marcy and me a few times. They'd liked her, and they'd been as surprised as I was when it came out that the rackets had put her on to me.

I put the hard in my voice. "See much of her down at the booking desk? She tricking for a living now?"

"She's four-oh clean."

"That's great, and so am I."

"Edna's seen her a few times and she really likes her, and you know how Edna believes in sin."

"She also believes in repentance," I said. I wasn't sure that I did, and maybe that was one of my faults, one of the cracks in my dry clay.

"Edna went shopping with her last Saturday. Almost ruined me at Rich's and Davidson's." He stopped and waited, letting it hang there so that I could ask questions if I wanted to. I wasn't about to. I'd be damned if I was going to. "Rehabilitation got her started in social work. She spent almost a year in a short course up in North Carolina. Now she's working with the state."

"Why in Atlanta? It looks like she'd have gone somewhere where she wasn't known."

"Exactly," Art said, and turned and looked at me.

So Art had outplayed me after all, and the circle was closed, and for all my hard shell, I got the blow solid in the guts. I leaned back and closed my eyes against the slanting glare of the winter sun. I had nothing more to say until we reached Millhouse.

The stakeout was still in place down the street from the wooden frame house where the Spences lived. Two bored small-town cops, almost asleep in their patrol car. It was a hundred yards down the street, pointed toward the Spence house. When Art saw the marked car with the red light on top he began to steam. "That's like announcing it in the papers."

We parked nose to nose with the Millhouse Police car and Art walked over and showed his I.D.

"Chief Brunson said you were coming," the cop in the driver's seat said. "You can go on up."

Art kept his temper. "Maybe one of you ought to come along with me. I don't have any jurisdiction here in Millhouse."

"Oh, sure." The one in the driver's seat got out quickly, and we crossed the street and angled toward the Spence house. The house needed paint, but it looked like it got the kind of care that costs only sweat and effort. There were flower boxes on the porch railings, neat and waiting for the spring. A porch swing creaked in the December wind. Two porch rockers were covered with sheets of plastic taped in place. From the height of the porch, I could look in all directions and see that the Spence lawn was raked clean of leaves, while the lawns in all directions looked yellow-brown with leaf clutter.

The Millhouse cop reached past me and knocked on the door.

Mrs. Spence was probably in her late forties, but she looked ten years older. She stood in the open doorway and wiped her hands on a damp apron. Her hands were big-boned and so red that I might have marked it down to the dishwater, if her face hadn't had that same kind of weathered and mistreated look.

When the Millhouse cop told her who we were, she hesitated just a moment before she asked us in. As she turned away, I saw that her hair was pulled back into a skin-tight bun, like the kind my grandmother used to wear. And then, as we went inside, I saw her husband seated in a rocker beside an old oil heater. Even seated, he looked tall and knob-boned, like all the spare flesh had been sliced off him.

I thought I knew both well, even before they said their first words. They were farm people, out of place in town. They probably didn't have a single friend on the street, or in the whole town. But stop by her door and she'd ask you in with warmth, and if you hadn't eaten she'd feed you the best she had in her kitchen. Perhaps even better than she ate herself. But with Art and me it was different. We were hunting her son, and that put a cold wind in the house. We were going to get the country politeness that she gave people she didn't like or approve of.

Mr. Spence got up from his rocker, and habit almost got the better of him. For a moment I thought he was going to offer us his hand. Instead, catching himself, he rubbed the palm against his thigh, as if trying to scrape something from it, something sticky that didn't want to be rubbed away.

I opened my topcoat to the oil heater and warmed myself. Art did his questioning. *No, they hadn't heard from Eddie since Chief Brunson came by on Wednesday night. The last time they'd heard from him was the day after he moved to Atlanta. He'd called that afternoon and talked to her, and had given her the name of* the hotel and the phone number there. *He said he was all right, and he had some leads on jobs. No, they'd never been to Atlanta in their whole lives, and they certainly hadn't met any friends he might have there. Yes, Eddie had talked about having one friend there, but he didn't say his name, and he didn't say what the friend did for a living.*

Then, with obvious pain at saying something they knew would hurt Eddie: *Yes, he did have a pistol, one he brought back from his time in the service. He said the Navy let him keep it. She had seen it in his dresser drawer and had asked him about it. It was kind of square-looking and blocky.*

Art got out his pad and drew a quick sketch of a .45. He showed the sketch to Mrs. Spence and then to her husband. *Yes, that was what it looked like. It certainly did. Yes, he'd fired it a few times. He said it was just for target practice, anyway. One time, Eddie and some of his friends had chipped in and bought a box of bullets, and they'd done some target shooting out behind the pool hall. Eddie said he won ten dollars at it from that Sharp boy, the one whose daddy ran the pool hall. Well, he had been in trouble once for firing the gun at the drive-in movie, but the other man had started it by talking smart to Eddie and to the girl he was with. Chief Brunson had asked Eddie about the gun, but Eddie had lied and said he threw the gun in the lake after he left the drive-in.*

I could see that Art had just about finished his questioning. I backed away from the oil heater and went over to stand beside Art. It was my turn. *Yes, Eddie had gone with Emily Campbell all through high school, up to his senior year. That was back in Mason, before Eddie went into the service and they had moved to Millhouse. They had stopped going together because her father, Mr. Arch Campbell, didn't like it one bit.*

Eyes curving their signal past me when I asked what Arch Campbell had done to break up Eddie and Emily. *Came to them out on the piece of land he owned that they were working on shares for him, and he said that if Eddie didn't stop seeing his daughter right* away, he was going to put his lawyer to work to break the lease. He could get a court order so they'd have to stop working the land until the judge made his decision, and if the crop rotted in the ground it didn't matter to him. It didn't matter to him how much it cost him in crop loss, or lawyers' fees, or court costs, he'd do it.

The poor man's sense of pride and outrage spitting out. So they talked to Eddie the first chance they got, and he would have stopped seeing that Campbell girl, but she kept after him, wouldn't obey her father and wouldn't let him obey his mother and father. Eddie was seeing her in secret until Mr. Arch Campbell found out about it and did his next dirty trick. He waited his time and had Eddie arrested for drunk and disorderly, when Eddie never in his life had as much as one beer. And they said he resisted arrest, and they beat him on the chest and stomach until he was more blue than he was white. It wasn't long after that when Eddie dropped out of school and went into the service, all the way out in California. If he ever saw that girl again, then he was the Lord's biggest fool.

I nodded at Art that I was through. Art thanked the Spences for their time, and we started for the door. Even as I went with him, I knew that it wasn't going to be that easy. It wasn't. Mrs. Spence scurried around us and blocked the doorway.

"What are you going to do with Eddie?"

Behind us, Mr. Spence was trying to shush her.

"No, I want to know. I'm his mother, and I've got a right to know, if anybody has."

"It's up to him," Art said. His face was flushed, and he was having trouble getting the words out. "If he'll give himself up, he'll get a fair trial."

"And if he won't?"

Art shook his head. There wasn't any way he could tell her, but she already knew. It was there in her face for us to see, in the same way that she could read our faces and know. She stepped out of the doorway a lot slower than she moved there, and Art and I and the Millhouse cop walked out of the dry heat into the cold wind. Behind us, after the door closed, we could hear her voice rising, rising, and his low, muffled voice, and it wasn't until we crossed the road and reached the Millhouse patrol car that we had it blotted out, and I could take a deep breath again.

CHAPTER NINE

Chief Branson, fat and grotesque, wheezing like he was seconds away from a heart attack, met us at Sharp's pool hall with the sheriff and one of his deputies. We'd had the stakeout cop call him from the patrol car, and the chief had said it would take him the better part of an hour to work it out with the sheriff, but he'd meet us there. Art and I took that hour to have supper in one of the greasy spoons downtown. Even taking our time, we got there a few minutes before the chief's car led the sheriff's into the parking lot. Sheriff Dawson wore a pearl-handled pistol on his right side, butt forward. He got out of his car and swaggered over to us like he could outdraw the whole lot of us.

Art introduced himself and showed his I.D. He told the sheriff what he wanted, and the sheriff went inside the pool hall and came out a minute later with Marshall Sharp, the pimply kid that Hump and I had talked with two nights before. The kid remembered me but didn't speak. The deputy came over carrying a Coleman lamp and a couple of flashlights. Then the sheriff. Art and the deputy followed the kid around the building and into the woods beyond.

Chief Brunson and I had decided not to go. The chief said all this area was out of his jurisdiction, and I said it looked a little warmer inside the pool hall. We nodded at each other and went inside.

The same bartender was there. He'd been working over things to say to me, but when he saw I was with the chief, all he said, in a friendly voice, was, "Didn't bring any niggers with you tonight?"

In an equally friendly voice, I said that all the black players from the Falcons, the Hawks, the Braves and the Chiefs would be dropping by in the next fifteen minutes or so. Hump'd told them all how nice and friendly the pool hall was. "I hope you've got enough cold beer for about a hundred mean and thirsty black men."

"We got other things for 'em, too," the bartender said, moving away to leave Chief Brunson and me to drink our beers.

"The Spence boy's got himself in a lot of trouble, huh?" the chief asked.

"As bad as there is."

"You can't tell about these kids, nowadays," the chief said, mock-sadly. "I knew he was a mite wild, but I thought I'd straightened him out."

I asked him how well he knew Eddie.

"Well enough to let him work on my car. He had the makings of a damned good mechanic."

When we finished the first beer, the chief nodded at the bartender and he brought two more. He pushed my hand away from my wallet and said. "It's on my tab." I let it go, seeing that it was part of his small-town graft.

"Eddie have many friends here in Millhouse?"

"Not many. He didn't grow up around here, you know. There was just Marshall Sharp and two others that he ran around with most of the time."

"The other two still in town?" I asked.

"Come to think of it, they aren't," the chief said. "The Eaton boy, he got drafted back in October. Last heard from, he was out in Oklahoma. The other boy, named Clinton Stubbs, he just drifted off a month or two ago, and I never heard where he went."

I got out my pad and wrote down *Clinton Stubbs*. "What'd he do for a living?"

"He was a mechanic, just like Eddie Spence. Worked at the same shop here in town, Allgood's."

I added that to my pad. *Mechanic.*

We were on our fifth beer when Marshall Sharp came in looking chilled and put out. The chief and I gulped down what was left in our glasses and went outside. The sheriff and his deputy were backing out of the lot when we reached Art. Art thanked Chief Brunson and said he'd buy him a drink when he came to Atlanta. I waved at the chief and belched politely, and Art and I got into his cruiser and headed back to Atlanta.

"We got four pretty good slugs out of a tree," Art said. "We'll see if they match up with the ones we took out of the patrolman in the alley behind the hotel."

That made sense. That was in case Eddie got rid of the gun.

I wrote down *Clinton Stubbs—Mechanic* on another sheet of paper and passed it to Art. "This is one of Eddie's two friends. He left town about a month or so before Eddie did."

"From the chief?"

I said yes.

"Shit, we asked him and he didn't know anything."

"You weren't drinking with the rank old bastard," I said.

"Thank god."

While I dialed Information, Hump brought me a beer from the refrigerator. After a few seconds of searching, the operator said there wasn't a number listed for a Clinton Stubbs. I marked that off. One down.

Hump slouched in front of the TV. "You look on the rag."

"I am, and it's hard flow." I sat next to Hump and watched part of a war movie while I gave Art time to drive to his office at the department. I was jumpy and pissed off, and I'd been thinking about Marcy all evening, ever since Art had tossed her back at me. It hadn't been easy, but I thought I'd weeded her out for good.

Art answered on the second ring. "Jim, I thought I got rid of you for the night."

"Nothing on Clinton Stubbs at Information," I said.

"I didn't think it would be that easy."

"Gas, water and electricity... that might be the way," I said. "You can do without a phone, but not lights, heat or water."

"I'll check it first thing in the morning, when the offices open."

"I could do that myself, if I wanted to wait that long." I let that hang a moment. "Look, twelve hours might be the difference between catching Eddie and letting him slip away."

"If he's in town in the first place," Art said. "If Clinton Stubbs is even in town. If Eddie's staying with Clinton Stubbs."

"He's got to be staying somewhere. You got a better guess?"

"Not at the moment."

"There must be somebody at the emergency numbers. Use your cop clout."

I heard him suck in a deep breath. "All right. You going to be at Hump's?"

I turned to Hump. "We going to be here?"

Hump made the cupped hand motion for a drink.

"No, we'll be at the Hut."

The Hut is an old warehouse-turned-into-a-bar, out in the direction of Emory University. It was an "in" place for Emory students for a year or so, and when they stayed away in droves at another, new "in" place, the owner decided to angle it toward the pleasures of the middle thirties... drinking and chasing. There were usually ten or twelve unescorted women around most nights, office girls looking for love without romance, and the drinks as far as we could tell weren't watered.

Now and then, when the pressure gets to me and I'm past feeling like a hawk or a scavenger, I walk off with one of the girls and we grunt and roll around like a ballet for large, awkward fish, and then I put on my pants and go home, weakened and a little bit sad.

I took a booth away from the front door and out of the occasional blast of outside air. Hump walked to the bar, looked over the rest of the sparse crowd, and came back to the booth. "Nobody here I know."

"Or want to know?"

"There's one horse over there, a blonde with a winter tan that makes her almost as dark as I am."

"Alone?"

A waitress brought over our drinks, double scotches.

"Some college-looking kid with her," Hump said.

"Too bad." I gulped at my drink and looked up, and saw Hump staring at me. "What's wrong?"

"You're drinking it like it was poisoned."

I thought about it a second and nodded. "That might be. Eddie Spence's mother and father got to me. Good people who worked themselves humpbacked making a living. Now it turns out they've got a son who thought he was going to be Cinderella-boy. Going to marry the rich boss's daughter. Going to live in a big house, and screw and eat ice cream all day."

"Then something's missing in that boy," Hump said.

"Huh?"

"… if he killed that girl?"

"Don't people kill people they love?" I asked.

"I've got a feeling you're not talking about that Spence boy at all."

"You know too much." I tried the drink again, tasting it this time. He did know too much. He'd been around when the Marcy King thing broke open. I'd been in pretty bad shape, and it was about that time that I started to think of Hump as a friend. He always seemed to be around when I was about to get my ass whipped by four rednecks, or about to do my drunken pratfall in front of a car.

"Enough," Hump said, "I know enough."

"Marcy call you lately?"

"Who? Me?"

"You," I said.

"Just to ask how you were. How your soul was."

"What'd you say about my soul?"

"Dark. Dark and full of ashes."

While I was worrying that around in my mind, the waitress came over and said I had a call at the bar phone.

"Right the first time," Art said. "Everybody needs electricity." He gave me an address on Monroe Drive. They were putting together a raiding party, and I was invited if I got there in time.

Hump drove. He knew ways through the town that I didn't. With some of the dark streets looking alike, I was lost until we reached Virginia-Highland. We followed Virginia until it ran into Monroe Drive. There, where Virginia petered out, we faced Grady High School. Hump took a left and headed in the direction of Ponce De Leon.

"There."

He took a sharp right onto Eighth, and pulled up behind a patrol car and two unmarked cars. As I got out of the car I could look past a tear in the canvas cover on the fence and see one endzone on Grady field. A nervous-looking uniformed cop with a riot gun met us on the sidewalk. "You want something?"

Art detached himself from a small group and came over to us. He waved the cop away. The cop moved out of hearing. "You're not carrying anything, are you? Either of you?"

Hump and I lied and said we weren't.

"Stay out of it then." He gave me the layout. Clinton Stubbs had a small apartment just a few doors down from Eighth and Monroe. It was the gray frame house with green trim and the

APARTMENT FOR RENT sign out on the lawn. The whole block was sealed off. One car was back on Charles Allen Drive, the street one block over and parallel to Monroe. Another car was stationed on the Circle on the block side facing Ponce De Leon. Two cops would stay with the cars on Eighth and close off that side. That left only the Monroe Drive side, and we would be going in from that direction.

"The problem is," Art said, "that we don't have any real worthwhile description of Stubbs." He'd called Chief Brunson, and the one he gave would fit half the guys in the raiding party.

"So you've got to catch him in the apartment, or run the chance of missing him."

"That's it," he said.

Counting Hump and me, there were eight in the party. No matter how quiet we tried to be as we walked down Monroe, it sounded like a company of soldiers breaking step on a wooden bridge.

At the house the party broke up into their assigned positions, one uniformed cop covering the back and one on each side. The nervous young cop who'd met Hump and me earlier was out on the sidewalk facing the front of the house, a riot gun at the ready. Hump and I stood with him and watched as Art and another plainclothes detective worked their way up the front steps to the porch. They crossed the porch and went through a screen door, then another door, and then probably into a hallway. There would be steps there that led up to the second floor and the Stubbs' apartment, which was on the front right-hand corner of the building. The windows were dark there, and I hoped that everyone in there had had a few drinks and was deep under. As soon as they'd gone past the screen door, I started counting. When I'd reached three minutes and thirty-four seconds, it went bad. The lights went on in the Stubbs apartment. At that, the cop next to me clicked off the safety on his riot gun.

"Steady," I said to him, "I'll tell you when."

"Look, mister…" The anger was there, but so was about a hundred-pound lump of fear.

"When *I* say so," I said, as firm as I could be under the circumstances.

The window toward us rasped open, and the shape of a man blotted out the lighted square for just a moment. And then he was gone, and the light was whole again. The man, whoever he was, was coming down the corner drain pipe. About halfway down, the pipe pulled away from the house, bending with a rusty creak, and the man fell into the yard. He landed on his side, and then he was up and running toward us.

"Stop and put up your hands!" I shouted at him. For a split second he did exactly that, just long enough for me to see that he wasn't armed. Then he changed his mind and angled away. Beside me, the riot gun was moving down from its skyward position. "Don't shoot! He's not armed!" But the riot gun was still moving down, and I gave Hump a shove toward the fleeing man. "Get him." Then I turned on the young cop and caught the barrel of the riot gun and pushed it upward. At the same time I moved close to him and gave him a hip check that shook him and the gun apart. When I looked back around, Hump was bearing down on the man. He hit the man about neck high, and they bounced once on the dirt and rolled over, and Hump was on top, sitting on him and holding his head down into the dirt.

I gave the cop back his riot gun. "Go arrest him, or something."

When Art came down a few seconds later, Hump was looking up into the circle of riot guns and saying, "Ease up, this mother ain't going anywhere."

"Where's Eddie Spence?"

"I don't know any Eddie Spence." Clinton Stubbs, hands cuffed behind him, was sitting on the edge of one of the kitchen chairs and glaring at us. His face was dirt-streaked and he was wearing a t-shirt, an oil-stained pair of jeans, and loafers without socks. He was smaller and thinner than he'd seemed out in the dark yard.

"That's not what Chief Brunson says."

"Chief Branson's a sack of shit."

I left Art and the other detective in the kitchen with Stubbs and went into the bedroom. Off to the right, in the bathroom, Hump was trying to get the dirt stains off the knees of his trousers. "Anything in there, Hump?"

"Two wet towels. Either two people took showers, or he took two showers."

I looked around the bedroom. The blankets were kicked back in a heap, and the sheet was dirty brown. In one corner of the room there was a pile of dirty shirts and underwear. I opened the dresser drawers. In one drawer there was a neat stack of starched shorts and t-shirts. In another there were three starched sport shirts and a mass of white cotton socks. That didn't tell me much.

I prowled around the rest of the room and reached the wastebasket beside the bed. Among the other odds and ends I found a large, balled-up piece of brown wrapping paper. It had strips of wrapping tape on it, and it looked like it had come from a bundle of laundry. When I spread out the paper, a large piece of white paper fell out. It was a sales ticket from Bill's Salvage Store:

6 s. @ .20	1.20
6 t. @ .20	1.20
4 s.s. @ .50	2.00
	———
Total	4.40

The sale was dated the day before, on the sixteenth. While I was studying the ticket, Hump came in from the bathroom. He was drying his hands on a large wad of toilet paper.

"You know a Bill's Salvage Store?"

"It's a store in the wino district. Sells laundry and cleaning that doesn't get picked up after three or four months." He took the ticket and looked down at it. "It looks like somebody bought six shorts, six t-shirts and four sport shirts."

I went back to the dresser. The starched shorts were size 34 and the t-shirts were 40's. The sport shirts in the other drawer were all marked large. I returned to the pile of dirty laundry and dug around in it with the toe of my shoe. I speared a pair of shorts size 30 and a dress shirt with a 14 neck.

I called Art in from the kitchen. I showed him the ticket and told him what I'd found. "Eddie left the hotel in a hurry. No time to pack spares."

Art nodded. I followed him into the kitchen and watched as he circled Stubbs. He grabbed the neck of Stubbs' t-shirt and pulled it away. "A 36," Art said to me.

Hump and I stood around and watched while Art went to work on Stubbs. He started out on neck sizes and shirt sizes, and when Stubbs insisted that all the shirts were his, Art made fun of him for swelling up and shrinking from day to day. The topper came when Art had the cuffs taken off him. He asked Stubbs to try on one of the large sport shirts I'd found. He didn't want to, but two of the cops put one of the sport shirts on him. He stood around and laughed at him, at the way the oversized shirt hung on him.

After a few minutes of that, Stubbs was ready to talk. Eddie Spence had shown up at his apartment the morning after the shooting at the hotel. Stubbs said he hadn't known about the shooting until he got to work and heard two of the other mechanics talking about it. That evening, when he asked Eddie about it, Eddie had said that one of the other cops had shot that patrolman by mistake in the dark, and they were trying to pin it on him. Stubbs had believed him, and Eddie had stayed on. And he'd bought some stuff from the salvage store because the only clothes he had were getting a little ripe.

The last time he'd seen Eddie? This morning, when he left for work at the body shop. And that was the Lord's truth.

Art left one policeman in the apartment and two others in an unmarked car in a driveway across the street. Hump and I waited around while Art made the arrangements, and then we followed them down to Eighth Street, where the cars were parked. After they put Stubbs in the back of a patrol car and before they closed the door on him, I leaned in.

"Did Spence say why he was staying in town?"

"I told him he ought to leave," Stubbs said.

"Did he say?"

"He said he had to get even with some people."

"Did he say which people?" I asked.

"No, just some people." He leaned back and crossed his legs at the knee. "What's your name?"

"Hardman."

Stubbs nodded. "I think he's looking for you."

CHAPTER TEN

H ump said, "You keep a messy kitchen, Hardman."

"What?"

"I can smell it all the way in here."

It was noon on Saturday, the day after the raid on Clinton Stubbs' apartment. It was a clear, cold morning, and Hump and I had driven over to my house to pick up a change of clothing. It was oppressively hot in the living room, and I caught a whiff of it, too, but I hadn't been sure what it was.

"I guess I didn't put out the garbage."

In the kitchen, the smell was even stronger. And then I saw what it was. The kitchen table was loaded down with pickles, olives, a couple of kinds of cheese, an open foil package of sliced roast beef, and a large mound of lox. Closer up, I could see that someone had tried the lox, hadn't liked it, and had spit out the piece he'd been chewing. The partly chewed wad of lox was on top of about half a pound of Nova Scotia.

"That boy's childish," Hump said.

"Or scared to where he doesn't give a damn." I got out a large trash bag and dumped his leftovers into it. "But at least, now we know where he spent yesterday and last night."

When I came back from the garbage dock, Hump was calling me. "In here, in the bedroom."

Hump was seated at the foot of the bed. He pointed at the large dresser mirror. Spence had written a message on it, using the wet edge of a piece of soap. I DIDN'T KILL EMILY. I WANT TO TALK TO YOU. E.S.

"This was on the floor." Hump held up a blue denim shirt. "And this on the bed." It was the plastic cover and shirt board from a laundry. "It looks like he swapped you a shirt."

The closet door was partly open. I pushed it the rest of the way, and spent a minute or two sliding the jackets and suits around. A gray Harris tweed jacket was gone, and so was a blue raincoat. "Well, he's got good taste in my clothes. How'd he get in?"

Hump nodded at the bedroom window that faced out into the backyard. As soon as I got close enough I could feel the cold draft from outside. A pane was missing. He'd tapped it out, reached in, and unlocked the window catch.

"That boy's learning bad habits."

I was stripping the sheets from the bed when the phone rang. It was Hugh Muffin.

"I've been trying to reach you for two days. You don't watch out, I'm going to quit paying you." He laughed. "How's it going?"

I told him we'd missed Eddie again the night before. He was lucky, but the luck would change.

"I went to Emily Campbell's funeral day before yesterday."

I didn't know what to say. I let the silence say it for me.

"Arch remembers the Spence boy, after all. He says he never was any good. The Mason police got him for drunk and disorderly while he was still in high school."

"That's not the way I heard it from the Spence family. The 'D and D' was a frame, and a beating went along with it, to tell the kid to stay away from Emily."

Hugh snorted into the phone. "A dead daughter is a hell of a price to pay for keeping the blood lines neat." He paused. "The reason I called. Ben Coleman wants to talk to you."

"Who?"

"Ben Coleman, Arch's business manager. You met him at the Regency that time."

"Yeah." I remembered him. He hadn't seemed to care much for me at the time. I couldn't think of anything I'd done that would make him change his mind. "What does he want?"

"I don't know." Hugh gave me the number. "Keep in touch."

Hugh hung up, and I dialed the number. A woman answered and stirred me, and called him to the phone. "I need to talk to you, Hardman."

"What about?"

"I'd rather not talk on the phone," he said.

"I'm busy."

"This is important, and it might be worth your time."

I didn't like it, but I agreed to meet him for a drink. He let me pick the place, and I picked a topless bar on West Peachtree, just for the hell of it.

I finished with the bed and then threw some underwear, socks and shirts into a suitcase. I changed into a fresh suit and put the one I'd been wearing since Thursday into the cleaning bag.

Hump sat on the edge of the bed and smoked. "The way you were talking to old Hugh, you don't sound as mad at Eddie as everybody else does."

"It's all so fucking dumb and useless, the whole thing."

Hump nodded at the writing on the mirror. "You believe that?"

"Too many people lie face to face for me to put much stock in mirror writing."

"But if it's true?" Hump asked.

"You believe him?"

"I've never met the dude," Hump said.

"That's the problem. Neither have I." I lifted the suitcase, and we went into the living room. "But I'd like about ten minutes with him. I need some answers. What bothers me is that Spence might be after The Man, and he might be after me. If this whole mess goes back to a high school romance…"

"The father," Hump said.

"He'd be my first choice. He's the one crapped on paradise. Arch Campbell himself."

"Unless we've got it all wrong," Hump said. "All the pieces have to fit together, and if they don't, that means we don't have all the pieces."

"That's reassuring," I said. I turned down the thermostat as low as it would go and we headed downtown.

We loafed over a light lunch and a second and third beer. I pushed the plates aside and, because of what Hump had said about the pieces, I got out my pen and pad. I began to list the possibilities.

1.   Eddie killed Emily C. because of the old romance. He wants to kill The Man for the same reason. Why not Arch C. also?

2.   Eddie killed Emily C. but for some reason not connected with the old romance. He wants to kill The Man for that same reason, whatever it is.

3.   Eddie killed Ferd because he saw Ferd with Emily. That would go back to #1.

4.   Eddie killed Ferd for some reason not involved with Emily C.

When I paused, Hump reached across the table and picked up the pad. He read what I'd written and then looked at me, his face closed and bland. "For somebody with a lot of sympathy for Eddie, you're missing about half of it."

I handed him the pen. "Write a few."

Hump spent a few minutes writing, then pushed the pen and pad back across the table to me.

5.   Eddie did not kill Emily C. If he didn't, then maybe he thinks The Man did, or you did.

6. *If Eddie didn't kill Emily C., then why would he kill Ferd?*
I looked up from the pad. Hump was grinning at me.
7. *Somebody else killed Emily C. and Ferd. Why?*
8. *Two different people killed Emily C. and Ferd, for different reasons. Who?*
9. *Back to #6. Eddie didn't kill Emily C. but he killed Ferd because he thought Ferd had something to do with Emily's death.*
I closed the pad and put the pen away.

"The first mistake was natural enough," Hump said. "You just wanted to question Eddie about Emily. No proof of any kind that linked him to it. But he flipped out and shot the cop in the hotel alley. Then the logic got all screwed up. *Eddie is a killer. He killed a cop. Therefore he also killed Emily Campbell. Therefore he killed everybody* who's *been killed lately and everybody who gets killed next week.*"

"We got locked into it too early," I said.

"Locked in tight," Hump said.

I bought the lunch. It was the least I could do after being stupid.

We parked in the lot about half a block from the Pirates' Cove on West Peachtree. It had a clapboard front painted sort of driftwood brown, and there was a topless girl in a pirate's outfit and an eye patch painted on the sign that hung over the sidewalk. It was five of two, and the place had just opened, but there was the smell of warmed-over stale beer and cigarette smoke in the heating system.

There were two convention types at the bar having pick-me-ups. Otherwise, it was empty. Hump and I took a table near the low performer's platform, and the bartender came over and took our orders. When he brought our beers, he clipped us a buck and a half each for them and, perhaps to soften that, said the go-go girls would be starting up soon.

"Why this place?" Hump asked.

"You never see enough titties," I said, and let it go at that.

❧   ❧   ❧

Ben Coleman came in around ten after two. The first go-go dancer was on, a fat blonde girl with skin that had the color and dull sheen of biscuit dough. Her breasts were like soggy dumplings that had been cut out with a quart jar top. As soon as I saw Ben Coleman's dark hair and aggressive walk, I started clapping for the fat girl. Hump looked at me like I was going crazy, but I nodded at him and he joined in. The fat girl thought we were crazy, too, but it was better than being ignored altogether. "Whip it, sugar."

A waitress, one of the other dancers, followed Coleman over to our table and took his order for a Jack Daniels Black, on the rocks.

Coleman looked irritated. "Hardman, I…"

"You mind waiting until this pretty lady finishes?"

"Lady…?" He gave the blonde a sour look. "Hardman, I called you for a good reason, and…"

"Coleman, this is my partner, Hump."

Hump and Coleman nodded at each other. Coleman said, "Is this your idea of some kind of a joke?" His drink came and he looked at it and paid for it, but he didn't touch it. "I'm too busy to spend my time…"

He broke off because I wasn't listening. I was getting out a five and passing it to Hump. "Stuff her for me, Hump." Holding the bill out in front of him, Hump went over to the fat girl, waved it at her and, when she smiled and pulled out the front part of her bikini bottom, he folded the bill and dropped it into the opening. The elastic popped back into place, and Hump came back to the table. "Fat girls appreciate little kindnesses like that," he said, winking at me.

"Shit," I said, "it's only money."

"It's money I wanted to talk to you about," Coleman said.

"Really?" I looked at him and then away, up to the platform where the blonde was finishing up and blowing Hump and me kisses. Hump blew one of the kisses back at her, and I reached up and fielded one like a low, hot line-drive.

Coleman was getting angry. "Aren't you interested in money, Hardman?"

I mugged over at Hump. "Are we interested in money this week?"

"This is the week for trim," Hump said. "You remember? We said last week was for money."

"Right."

"Are you two crazy or something?"

The platform lights dimmed, and the loud music went down a notch or two. "All right," I said, "tell us about money."

"That's more like it." He waved his glass at the waitress and I held up a beer bottle and two fingers. "Since the funeral Thursday, friends of Arch Campbell have been getting together a reward fund. The last figures I saw, it was almost ten thousand dollars, and it might go as high as fifteen."

"Arrest and conviction?"

"Yes," Coleman said. "That's the way it'll be worded."

"That's good news, isn't it, Hump?"

"I could use a cut of it," Hump said.

"I just thought you might want to know," Coleman said. Then he leaned back, waiting for his drink and waiting to be thanked.

"A lot of money," I said.

Coleman was expansive now. "I was at the meeting when part of the reward was collected. Mr. Campbell and others as much as said that the reward would be paid whether Eddie Spence went to trial or not."

"You mean…?"

"He might resist arrest and get killed. If it happened that way, it might be easier for everybody concerned."

"Everybody but Eddie Spence," I said. "You see, we know that Eddie killed the cop out behind the hotel. No doubt about that. But we're beginning to wonder if he killed Emily Campbell."

Coleman looked astounded.

"So far, it's just a hunch," I said. "Nothing to hold it down. Just a feeling."

"But the police seemed so sure, and you seemed so sure..."

"Right now, until we're really sure, that reward is just a lot of blood money, and a lot of trouble."

"And wrong-man blood money, at that," Hump said.

"That kind of money draws flies," I said.

The drinks came. Coleman sipped at his. "What do you mean by *flies?*"

Hump gestured with his beer glass. "Every small town stud who always wanted to be a private eye is going to show up in Atlanta, packing the Saturday Night Special he borrowed from his cousin. Buddy. God, it'll almost be a convention of guys who read Travis McGee novels."

"That kind of money buys a Judas, and..."

"Judas?" Coleman broke in on me.

"Say you committed a murder, and your girlfriend knew about it. Somebody offers a fifteen-thousand-dollar reward for information leading to the arrest and conviction of the murderer. There's a good chance you'd end up minus a girlfriend, and she might end up plus fifteen thousand dollars."

"You think the reward's too high, then?" Coleman asked.

"No. It's not my place to say. It's their money, and they can spend it the way they want to." I stopped to top off my beer and take a long swallow. "But unless there's a Judas around, it's not going to speed up things one damn bit."

"I see." He looked put down.

"It's not your fault," Hump said. "It's just that there might not be anybody who knows enough to be the Judas."

Coleman looked at me, and then at Hump. "It seems this business is a lot more complex than I thought it was."

"With some luck, we might get a chunk of the fifteen thousand," I said. "Cheers."

"Cheers," Coleman said.

I sat back and belched politely into my hand. "How long have you been working for Campbell?" The way I put it, it was just talk among the boys.

"Three years ... a bit more."

"He an easy man to work for?"

"Sometimes, sometimes not. Just between you and me ..." He hesitated until I nodded that it was. "... he can be hell on hot wheels when he doesn't get his own way."

"I guess I can see that," I said.

"He's like a lot of those self-made men, the ones who drop out of school in the seventh grade and think they know all there is to know." A note of high sharpness had come in, and he smiled and shook his head, going back to being the little boy. "Of course, I don't want you to misunderstand me. He wouldn't be where he is now if he wasn't a pretty damn smart guy."

I thought we'd gone as far in that direction as it was worth. Hump leaned in and said, "You've been with him over three years, so I guess you were around when Eddie Spence was courting Emily."

"It was just one of those high school crushes. It wouldn't have lasted past her first year in college, but Arch wouldn't listen to reason."

"You tried to talk him out of it?" Hump saw me lift an eyebrow at him. That meant to carry it on, string it out.

"I did everything but beg him. But what worried him was the possibility that they might run off and get married before she got to college and met those handsome college men."

"How'd he handle it?" Hump asked.

"Just a phone call. The sheriff ... his name is Todd Blaney ... was happy to do a favor for Arch. There was a beer joint outside the city limits that sold beer to under-age kids. Eddie and some of the other boys hung out there. The sheriff just picked a night when Eddie was there, and came in and did some rough arresting. Maybe Eddie put up a struggle out in the parking lot, like they said. Maybe not. He got a bit of a beating, either way."

"How did Emily take all this?"

"She was mad, at first."

"And then?" I asked.

"Arch lied to her and said he hadn't had anything to do with it, that it had just been the sheriff enforcing the law, like he was elected to do."

"And she believed that?" Hump signaled the waitress for another round.

"Not right away. But then Eddie left town and ended up in the Navy, and not too long after that, she started dating other boys."

"Young love don't last long, does it?"

"About two jumps," I said.

Hump laughed and Coleman looked a little stunned, like he didn't understand.

It was my turn. "You look like a guy who's been around, Coleman. How did you see this Emily girl?"

"Young, very pretty, not as much sense as she'd have had in another year or two. Lord, she was a pretty little thing. Made your teeth ache, just to look at her."

"You ever take her out, Coleman?"

"Me? She was a little young for me."

"She wasn't that young," Hump said.

"You ever get any of it?" I asked.

That seemed to shock him. He pushed back his chair and stood up. "That's a terrible thing to say. You know that, don't you?"

"If it was so nice," Hump said, "I'd feel better knowing that it wasn't wasted."

"God, you two are a pair of ghouls."

"You didn't answer the question," I said.

Ben Coleman strode out of the bar with a heavy-footed, aggressive walk.

"You're right about one thing," Hump said. "He didn't answer the question."

The waitress brought over the round of drinks, including the Jack Daniels for Coleman. I paid for the drinks and Hump took the Jack Daniels, to sip along with his beer.

"At first, I thought you were being unkind to that poor fellow," Hump said.

"That's right," I said. "And after he came all the way down here, to tell us where the treasure was hidden."

"He seemed like such a nice, open fellow ... so honest."

"Right."

"But when I got to know him, I didn't like him very much," Hump said.

"That's the second time I didn't like him."

We sat around for a few more minutes and watched the next go-go dancer. It turned out to be our waitress, and she must have been new at it or extremely modest, because she didn't take off the top of her costume the whole time we watched.

On the drive back over to Hump's apartment, I made myself a note in my pad. *Find out relationship Emily and Coleman. Where was Coleman the night of murder?*

While I unpacked the clothing I'd brought from my house, I asked Hump if he was doing anything that evening. "Nothing the rest of the afternoon, and nothing this evening."

"I want you to cruise some of the black bars. Now that we're working on the assumption that Eddie didn't do it, let's touch all the other bases." Without pushing, I wanted him to find out anything he could about how The Man and Emily C. got along. Any recent trouble? How were things between The Man and Ferd? And with any free time left over after that, I wanted to know anything he could find out about The Man's organization.

"That could be rough, asking those questions in his home territory."

"That's why you're doing it instead of me, Tonto," I said. "Anyway, I've had my beating for the month."

Hump put on his coat "I might as well start now. The sooner I start, the sooner the bruises start healing."

"The word that we're working for The Man might cover you."

"Maybe. But not when you're asking questions *about* The Man."

He left, and I got a beer and sat and watched part of a college football game between a couple of Ivy League Schools. I was kind of sorry that Hump had left, because he'd have got a laugh out of the single-wing that Dartmouth was using. At five, I turned the sound down and called Art.

"News for you."

"If you've got any more wild-goose chases, you fly after them."

I told him about Eddie's note on the mirror.

"That's horseshit and you know it. The slugs from the tree behind the pool hall match the ones we took from Reese...the cop in the alley."

"That's the cop," I said. "Emily wasn't shot."

"Just a second." I could hear him talking with Edna away from the phone. In a few seconds he was back. "Edna says you're to come to supper. She's fixing a roast the way you like it, cooked in wine."

"I don't know whether I can."

"Come on," Art said. "She wants to see your homely face."

"As long as it's not my beautiful body." I said I'd be over around six-thirty.

On the way over to their place, I cut into Piedmont and followed it until I reached Ansley Mall. I stopped there long enough to visit the wine shop and buy a couple of bottles of Mouton Cadet. I knew it was a wine that Edna liked. Raising four kids on a cop's pay didn't leave much for even an inexpensive wine. I knew we'd probably only drink one bottle. The other bottle would make Edna happy one day next week.

I heard the tap, tap, tap as I was going up the front walk. I changed directions and cut across the lawn to the driveway. I followed the driveway and found Mickey, aged six, and Andrew, aged eight, playing one-on-one at the basketball hoop that Art and I had put up on the side of the garage a couple of years ago. They were so intent on the game that they didn't see me, and I stood and watched. Then Andrew got a rebound and dribbled out toward me. He saw me, stopped, and whipped the ball to me. I batted it down with my free hand and trapped it with one foot. I put the wine down to one side and dribbled over to the corner and did my one-hand jump. I missed the hoop and all.

"Hardman, you're out of shape," Mickey said.

"You're right." I got the wine and went up the back steps to the kitchen. Edna had her back to me, cutting up celery, carrots and green peppers at the cutting board. She is a red-haired woman in her early thirties, with wide hips and the shoulders of a swimmer. She has a flat, round Irish face, with about the bluest eyes I've ever seen. When she heard the door and turned and saw me, her hands were full of chopped vegetables. I lifted the top from the large skillet and leaned over it, smelling the winy liquid the roast was cooking in. She reached in to drop the vegetables in and I replaced the skillet top.

"Jim, it's good to see you." She gave me a firm hug, holding it for a long time, as if she wanted me to feel the warm flow from her to me. "It's been too long."

"I've been busy. You know how it is." But I couldn't meet her eyes when I lied to her.

"That's a lie, isn't it, Jim?"

"Yes."

"The way you left the force, you thought it would hurt Art if you hung around with him?"

"Yes."

"Nobody worth knowing believed that shit." Shit was a strong word for her to use. I'd never heard her say more than a lower-case damn now and then.

"Careful now," I said. "Tomorrow's Sunday."

"I mean it."

I took the two bottles of Mouton Cadet out of the bag and put them on the counter. "I don't have to work tonight. You and I can get a little tipsy, even if Art can't."

She grinned at me and I went through the dining room and into the living room, where Art was in his stuffed chair reading the *Journal.* I got out of my topcoat and sat down on the sofa.

Edna came in with two bottles of beer, "It's all done but the sauntering. I can sit with you for a minute."

"Where are the girls?" I meant Connie and Agnes, the oldest children. I'd been around when they were born, and I'd had to suffer with Art when it looked like he wasn't going to get the sons he wanted.

"A slumber party down the street." She sipped on Art's beer before she passed it on to him.

Art put down his paper when he took the beer. "You believe Eddie Spence, that he didn't kill Emily Campbell?"

Edna stood up. "If you're going to talk shop, I'll fix the salad."

"I don't know," I said. "But if it's true, it muddies the waters."

I heard the kitchen door close behind Edna.

"But why you? Why'd he go to the trouble?"

"I'm dogging him, and he doesn't like it."

"If he sets up a meeting with you," Art said, "you'll have to tell me in time to set it up so that we can take him."

I shook my head. "I want to know what he has to say."

"We'll take him after you're through talking."

"I don't think it'll work." I leaned toward him and made it as forceful as I could. "Look, he's scared and he's getting a lot of practice at running. If I see him at all, it's going to be without much warning. No time to stake out a place. He'll step out of a doorway with the safety off, and the cannon pointing at me. I don't love you enough to get killed for you."

"Try to talk him into coming in."

I nodded. I could do that. I didn't think he'd listen, but I could try.

Twenty minutes or so later, while Art was setting the table in the dining room, the door bell rang.

"Get that for me, will you?" Art said.

I went to the door and opened it. The breath went out of me like I'd been kicked.

Marcy King stood in the doorway, smiling at me.

CHAPTER ELEVEN

A wind blowing through the empty places in me. Sounds like the inside of a conch shell, or blowing over the edge of an empty jar.

Memory of a night in New York, a year ago. The newspapers playing hide-and-seek for me in Atlanta, while I hid, an airplane ride away. A call-girl I met there who looked like Marcy. The same blonde-toward-reddish hair, the same slim and fine-boned body, slate-gray eyes and pale skin that wouldn't tan ... but I couldn't get it up. Paid her anyway and, knowing why I'd wanted to ravage her, I fell off the edge. Set off on a nightmare week of bars and hotel rooms, the final night with the hiccups. Hiccupping through half the bars in the Village, one time so hard that the tie-tac flew out of my tie and hit the bartender in the face. Bleeding out of all the empty places then, leaving a spoor everywhere I went.

Until it didn't bother me anymore. I thought.

"Hello, Jim." Smiling, but there wasn't any sureness in the smile. Instead, a wavering at the corners of her mouth. "I'm supposed to say that I didn't know you'd be here, but I knew."

"Such careful honesty," I said.

"It's about time I was." The smile gone, replaced by a calm seriousness, waiting until I decided to do whatever it was I was going to do.

"Or I was. Or somebody was." Aware then of the stillness of the house, no rattling of silver or dishes, only in the distance, with the door open, the faint tap, tap, tap of the basketball.

And without meaning to do it, not knowing I was going to do it, I put out a hand and cupped the side of her face. "I guess we might as well let the matchmakers think they won one." I turned to let her pass, and I heard her answer, like a whisper, "Yes."

But Art wasn't in the dining room, where I thought he was. We found him in the kitchen with Edna, and when Edna saw we'd gotten past the first, the hardest part, she broke down and started crying. Marcy saw that and, nervous as she was already, she began to cry along with her.

Art and I got another beer out of the refrigerator and went into the living room. Art leaned back in his chair and crossed his legs. "You think you and I spend a lot of time planning and plotting on something like the Spence case? That's nothing. Nothing at all. Edna and Marcy've been putting in forty hours a week overtime."

"You involved in this?"

"All I did was answer one question."

"Yeah?"

"They asked if this would work, and I said if you didn't kill her in the first two minutes, it was probably love."

We drank both bottles of the Mouton Cadet, and it was a great dinner, and I couldn't remember it ever being better. Art had to leave, but Marcy and I stayed on. Marcy helped with the dishes, and I sat around the living room, talking to Mickey and Andrew about pro football. They knew I knew Hump, and they were saying wistfully that it would be nice if I'd bring him over sometime, so their mother could meet him. Even after the dinner dishes were stacked away, I found I was still hesitating. I didn't know exactly what to do next. But it was time to go. I wanted to be at Hump's place when he came back from his tour of the black bars.

"Give me a lift home?" Marcy asked.

"Sure." I helped her with her coat.

"I came in a taxi," Marcy explained, "just in case."

I followed her directions and drove far out along West Peachtree, and then into a maze of circles and dead-end streets. Then the trees disappeared, and there was nothing but blowing red clay dust. We'd reached the Mellon Heights Apartments. I stayed with the paved road and fought a few bad bumps and stopped, when she said to, in front of 14A. It was something like a small motel unit, but it had it's own small lawn, without any grass yet, and a porch that would hold two people if they didn't mind sitting a close together. Out of the car and standing on the porch, it looked like a desert with building blocks thrown about it at random.

"As you can see," Marcy said, handing me her apartment key, "it just opened."

"Yes."

"I was one of the lucky ones, believe me. They moved some people in before they even had the sewer lines hooked up."

"Tricky, very tricky." I opened the door and stepped aside to let her through. I wasn't sure what I was supposed to do next. And not knowing, I decided I'd better say good night and head for Hump's.

"How about some coffee, Jim?"

"If I can make a call."

She pointed toward the phone and went through a door in the rear of the apartment to what was probably the bedroom. I dropped my topcoat on the back of a chair and, standing, dialed Hump's phone number. It rang seven times and there was no answer. That worried me a little, but not enough to go rushing out to look for him. Hump could take care of himself. Also, there was always the chance that Hump had run into some trim during his bar crawl. That was more likely than anybody getting the best of him.

I sat on the sofa and waited and smoked a cigarette. The furniture seemed like a familiar old shoe to me and, when I saw the antique china cupboard, I knew that these were the furnishings from her other apartment. I went over to the cupboard and ran my hands over the scarred panel on the right side. I remembered that cupboard very well. It was solid oak and weighed about a ton. I'd moved it for her once and thought I was going to get a hernia.

"I had them in storage while I was out of town." Marcy closed the bedroom door firmly behind her and passed me on the way into the kitchen. "It cost a fortune I didn't have."

Just to be talking, to say something: "You might have found some friend who'd have kept them for you."

She seemed to take a long time to answer. She folded and creased and recreased the filter paper for the Chemex coffeemaker. "Like you, Jim, I didn't have any friends left."

Boom. Pow. There it was. We weren't going to walk around it on our tiptoes. The door was open, and I could walk in and draw blood if I wanted to. But I drew back from it, not sure if I wanted to slash and rip and gut. I nodded and walked over to the breakfast nook and sat down, my back to the back door, watching her. "That was a long time ago. Sometimes, when I think about it, I almost believe that it was something that somebody told me had happened to them."

"I can't get the same distance," Marcy said.

"Time," I said." It's just a matter of time."

When the coffee was measured and the water in the kettle began its first faraway rumble, she set out cups and the sugar bowl and a small pitcher of cream. I looked at the cream pitcher and up at her. She swept the cream pitcher from the table and put it back in the refrigerator.

"The girl next door…she's in advertising…takes cream with her coffee."

"Lots of men take cream with their coffee," I said.

"None that I know."

"You're still young," I said. "It can change."

She stood with her back to the kitchen counter, hardly moving, staring through me until the cap on the kettle began its high, thin whistle. She blinked then, and put her back to me. As soon as the water was dripping through the filter, she put the kettle aside and sat down across the table from me.

"Jim, why did you come in here tonight? You need a cup of coffee that bad?"

I shook my head. "I'm not sure."

"What do you expect of me?"

"I'm not sure of that, either."

"You used to be so sure of everything," Marcy said.

"That's time for you."

"And stop saying those stupid, vague things." Her voice was still under control, but there was an edge, a rough surface to it. "I'd rather you beat me, or stomped me, or kicked me. You still do beat and stomp and kick people, don't you?"

"I kicked somebody last Tuesday, but since then I haven't had anybody around worth kicking."

"That's the Jim Hardman I know." She smiled. "Now I feel like I'm not with a stranger." She looked at the Chemex and back to me. "I'm going to tell you a story, and I'm only going to tell it once. After that, I want your promise that you'll never ask me about it again."

"Do I get to ask questions?"

"Yes, after I finish. But ask all of them tonight. Agreed?"

"Agreed," I said.

"And no interrupting?"

I nodded.

"This is about us, the book, chapter and verse. I didn't set out to meet you. That was an accident. I went to the Upshaw party with Bill and Frances Rutledge, who lived next door to me at the Colonial Arms, and I didn't even know who you were when I met you. In fact, if first impressions meant anything, I wouldn't even be sitting here with you tonight. I thought you were the biggest slob and creep I'd ever met."

I could remember. I even remembered Bill and Frances Rutledge. I'd been in one corner of the living room, bored shitless by a short, plump woman who just wanted to flirt with me a bit to get her husband's attention away from one of those leggy blonde types. And past her, I'd seen Marcy enter with another couple. I knew she wasn't with Bill Rutledge. He didn't look like man enough for her, and I'd decided right on the spot that I was, and made my excuses to the plump lady and headed for her.

"Of all the clumsy pick-up attempts I've had to suffer through, that was the all-time low. *Lady, is that your blue Mustang out front? You left your lights on. Oh, it's not yours? Well, I'm Jim Hardman.*"

It wasn't that bad. It wasn't as bad as some I'd heard and some I'd used before. But her answer was the bone-crusher of the year. "I think you've got a pimple on your nose, Mr. Hardman."

"The next day I'd forgotten you, Jim, and it hadn't been hard. But someone had seen me there, and they'd seen you following me around. Marsh said he'd heard I'd made a conquest. And it turned out that you were someone they were interested in, and I was told to cultivate you, to see if you had a price. I didn't want to do it. I argued. But when Marsh said for you to do something, it was jump and do it. So I bumped into you again."

That was at Frenchy's Pub, a place on Spring Street, Where I usually had lunch. The party had been on a Friday, and on the following Wednesday I went in for my corned beef and potato salad, and someone was sitting at my favorite table, the one near the window. It was Marcy, and it hadn't been easy to get past the hard wall of disinterest that she put up to face strangers. But I pushed and pushed and knew when not to push, and soon we were meeting for lunch almost every day. From that, it wasn't far to the evening, and dinner and a movie.

"Now and then Marsh would ask how it was going, and I'd say that it didn't look too favorable, and he'd drop it for a few days. Finally, he put me in a corner and said, *yes or no, will he take?* And I said that I was pretty sure you wouldn't, and he said that was what everybody else thought, too, and I could drop you now, and thanks a lot."

I wanted to ask the question. Suddenly, though I hadn't thought about it for a long time, I knew when she'd been told she could drop me. It was a puzzling day, one that stood out for me for all the wrong reasons. "The Falcon-49er game. That's a statement, not a question."

"Yes," Marcy said, "the Falcon-49er game." The water had settled through the filter. She filled our cups and sat down again. "He said I could drop you on the Friday before the game. That was why I broke the dinner date that night. But you took it so well and didn't get mad, and I knew I'd have to make a production out of it to really break it off."

It had been a good game. The 49ers must have been favored by a touchdown or two, but the Falcons toughed it out and won in the last seconds, when the Frisco kicker missed a chip shot. It should have been something to shout about, but it wasn't. Marcy had been distant from the beginning, hardly speaking to me, only yesses and noes when she did speak. Until, by the end of the game, I knew what she was trying to tell me. I remember it hit me while I was crossing the parking lot, and I wanted to die right then. I thought, *overmatched yourself this time, son,* and I started trying to write it off as a loss. Taking her back through the happy crowds, back to her apartment in a dead silence. Leaving her at the door when I'd planned to take her to dinner. Then back to my apartment and a bottle, finding the bottom of the bottle sometime after midnight. And a terrible hangover the next morning on the job.

"I found it wasn't that easy, Jim. I saw you were hurt but you took it well, and when you just said good night and didn't say anything about calling me, and you didn't say, *see you at Frenchy's,* I don't think I've ever felt quite as alone. But I thought it was something that would pass as soon as I went back to doing the usual things. I even went back to having lunch at the Brass Rail, where the other girls at the office ate."

I stayed away from Frenchy's for three days, and when I went in, Marcy hadn't been there. The waiter said he hadn't seen Marcy since the last time I'd brought her in.

"The first week I told myself it would get better. I'd just gotten used to having a man around."

As I'd gotten used to having a woman around.

"At the end of the first week, I took the first date offered me, a lawyer who ate with us now and then at the Brass Rail. But he wasn't much fun, and talked too much about how much money he was making, as if that would make me fall over backwards and drop my underpants for him."

Art and I went bowling three times that week. The third time I dropped him at his house, I heard Edna say something about this being the damned limit. After that I left Art alone and cruised some of the bars with Hump.

"And then one morning I woke up and looked at myself in the mirror while I was putting on my make-up, and I said *you think you're so smart, don't you? and let's see how smart you really are.* And that day I didn't go to the Brass Rail. I went to Frenchy's, and you didn't show up. The waiter said you'd been in the day before, but you weren't as regular as you used to be. Not every day, like you had been. And I went back the next day and the day after that, and finally you showed up."

I might not have gone back at all. Not ever, not ever. But the waiter, Harry, called me around noon and said, *that pretty lady is here now, and she asked about you, and I thought you might like to know.*

"From that moment on, from the time you came into Frenchy's, every word I said to you was true. Nothing held back. No lies. There were no reasons for seeing you that weren't my own personal reasons." Marcy got the coffee and topped off our cups. "Now you can ask your questions, Jim."

"I don't have any." I stood up and pushed back my chair. "I believe you. But second things first. I've got to call Hump." I left her and went into the living room. I dialed Hump's number. Still no answer.

When I came back to the kitchen, she was standing with her back to me, looking down at the table. Maybe, ass that I was, I hadn't realized that she'd been waiting for me to show and tell how things were between us now. And I'd left her to make a phone call. Damn me, anyway! I put my hands on her shoulders, and she turned so quickly it almost caught me off balance.

"I might still love you, Jim," Marcy said softly, "but you've changed. You're harder, and I'm going to need some time while I decide whether I still like you."

I said that was all right with me. And then I kissed her to see if we could jump over that year.

Hump was in his kitchen, soaking his right hand in a dishpan jammed with ice cubes. When he moved his hand it sounded like a cocktail party in progress.

"Trouble?"

"Some." He lifted his hand out of the ice water and flexed it. The knuckles were puffy and swollen. "Asking questions about The Man is not the way to be popular in that part of town."

"Any answers?"

"A few. The stud with the Afro was talking some until it dawned on him that I didn't seem to be asking the right kinds of questions. That was at the Dew Drop In Cafe." He took the hand out and dried it gently with some paper towels. "So I moved on, and it was right strange, but it seemed that everywhere I went, the stud with the Afro showed up. So, about half an hour ago, we had a few words out in a parking lot, and he hit me in the knuckles with the hard part of his head."

I got the J&B bottle down and a couple of glasses. We sat across from each other at the kitchen table. I poured while he talked.

"The Man's in everything... dope, pussy by the pound, gambling all the way from a dime on a number to thousands on a ball game. He's coining good money, and the word is that he's got clout that reaches all the way up to some political people. No names given. Just the suggestion that some big, big ones are slopping at his trough."

"Emily C.?"

"They had a thing going, hot and heavy. It was like she was trying to screw him to death. Some of his boys didn't like it much. They thought he was getting careless, letting her learn more about the operation than was good for her. But all the boys did was mumble to themselves some. Nobody was about to do anything about it. It was worth your hide to show any attitude toward her at all... good or bad."

"So there's no mourning among The Man's troops?"

"Not a bit." Hump laughed. "You see, there they are, his men, out prowling around with those pictures of Eddie, and the truth is that they're not sure whether they want to find him for The Man or give him a roll of cash, a pat on the back, and a way out of town."

"That might raise an ulcer or two."

"I don't think they're looking very hard." Hump carried his glass over to the refrigerator, looked in the ice chest, and then went over to the sink to fish a few chips of ice out of the pan he'd been soaking his hand in. "And not looking very hard might be as good a deal for Eddie as the cash and the pat on the back." He slumped into the chair and poured on some more J&B. "While I was out busting knuckles, what were you up to?"

I decided I might as well tell the truth. He would know it in a day or two, anyway. "I got caught between a couple of matchmakers and an old girlfriend."

Hump grinned. "Anybody get hurt?"

"Not that I know of."

"I'm glad for you." He toasted me with his glass. "Some other news. A flash on the radio a while ago said the town of Mason had put up a reward of twenty thousand dollars for the arrest and conviction of the murderer of Emily Campbell."

"It said the murderer, and it didn't name Eddie Spence?"

"That's right. There must be at least one lawyer in that group."

"But the heat's still on Eddie," I said.

"I wouldn't mind a part of that twenty thou."

I said I'd consider cutting him in. I finished my drink and got ready for bed. It was the first time in a long time that I slept the whole night without the anger and gall surfacing. There were no dreams at all that I could remember the next morning.

CHAPTER TWELVE

The next day was Sunday. I got up late, and Hump was padding around in the kitchen. I shaved and showered and dressed. In the kitchen, Hump handed me a cup of coffee and the sports page. "Welcome to the bright new world," he said.

"Do I look that way?"

"Not exactly, but I decided to say that this morning." He grinned at me. "What's on for today?"

"I'd like to talk to Eddie Spence."

"He's had a day or two to set it up. He's had time to pick a spot where he can't be staked out."

"So it might be today?"

"If he really wants to talk to you," Hump said.

"How'll he get in touch?"

"I'd say by phone. That's the way I'd do it. Too many people looking for him. Standing around on streets or in doorways, that's too much risk."

"Then maybe I'm at the wrong phone," I said.

"Might be."

I finished the coffee and Hump followed me into the living room. He watched while I got into my topcoat. "I'll be at my place."

"You want me along?"

I shook my head. "He might try here first."

"Watch yourself, Hardman."

I said I'd try.

The waiting seemed for nothing. I spent part of the time doing some chores around the house. I made up a laundry and a cleaning bag and put them by the front door, to be put out the next morning. I cut to size and taped in place a shirt board to fill in for the window pane that Eddie had broken. That would have to hold until I got a new pane in.

Around two, I found I was hungry, but there didn't seem to be much in the house. I hunted around and discovered a dusty can of black bean soup I'd bought on impulse a year or so before. I really wanted some lox or roast beef, but Eddie had ruined that. But the soup, when it was hot, was earthy-tasting, and I liked the faint trace of sherry in it.

There wasn't any pro ball on the tube. It was an open date before the conference championship games the next weekend. I watched a few minutes of a roller derby game, but got bored by the obvious phoniness. So I switched over to a history of the pro game, and laughed a little at the scratchy old footage and what seemed to be the jerky running styles of the backs.

At exactly four, the phone rang. It was Marcy. "Since you aren't going to call me, I thought I'd be the one to weaken."

I told her I'd been thinking about her, too.

"That's not enough. When do we start this marvelous courtship that every girl expects to tell her grandchildren about when she's seventy?"

I explained why I was waiting for a call.

"I'll believe you this time. Hump told me the same thing when I called him."

I got her phone number again and said that I'd give Eddie another hour and then give up on him. I'd call her then, and we could go out to dinner.

"Do I get to pick the restaurant?"

I said no.

She named a French restaurant just outside of town, one we'd gone to several times during the good days a couple of years before. "I've got a craving for something drowned in a beautiful sauce."

I said I'd try to come up with a French restaurant for her, but not that one.

"I think you're trying to tell me something."

That was for her to figure out, I told her. It just seemed to me, at that moment, that if we were going to start over, we might as well find ourselves some new bars and a new restaurant or two.

"It sounds like a hell of a courtship," she said, but she was laughing.

I said I wouldn't swear to that, but it was going to be the best one I could come up with.

Seconds after we broke the connection, the phone rang again.

"You're pretty long-winded, Hardman." It was a man's voice, but not one I knew.

"Who is that?"

"You know."

"I don't like guessing games," I said.

"You still eating that pink vomit?" He meant the lox, and I knew the caller was Eddie Spence.

"It went bad, left out of the refrigerator overnight."

"It was bad before that." A short pause. "I want to talk to you."

"I'm listening."

"No, face to face. You know the Music Museum in Underground Atlanta?"

"Yes."

"It'll take me thirty-five minutes to get there. I think it'll take you twenty-five. So you wait ten minutes before you leave the house. Got that, Hardman?"

"Yes."

"No tricks and no cops. If I see a cop, you're dead."

The line went dead.

Exactly ten minutes after he hung up on me, I left the house and walked along the stone walkway to the carport. My topcoat pocket felt strangely light: I'd decided against a gun. I wasn't paying much attention, just looking at the lawn and wondering if it was worth it to pay somebody to rake up the leaves. I opened the car door and looked into the barrel of Eddie's .45 automatic.

"Exactly on time."

"But the wrong place," I said.

"Let's ride around while we talk." He motioned with the .45, and I got in. "I called you from the service station a block away. I trust you about as much as I trust anybody, and that's not much."

"I didn't call the cops."

"We'll see." He'd dyed his hair a sort of reddish-brown, and he was trying to grow a mustache. It was just a wispy thing, a few days' growth so far. He was wearing my blue raincoat and the Harris tweed jacket I liked.

I backed out and turned. "Any special scenery you want to see?"

"Just drive." The gun was resting on his thigh, partly covered by a fold of the raincoat, but it was still pointed at me about stomach high. "I don't have a lot of time, Hardman."

"Talk then."

"I didn't kill Emily."

"Who did?" At the fork in the road, I selected the one going away from town.

"I don't know yet," Eddie said, "but she was afraid that somebody was going to."

"She tell you who it was?"

"No, and I asked her several times. But she was scared to death. She said it was because she knew something she wasn't supposed to."

"When was this?"

"The Friday before she was killed. I said I was coming to Atlanta to see if I could help her, but she said she didn't want me to."

That would be one of the calls from The Dew Drop In. And the "No, Eddie, no" that the stud with the big Afro heard. "And you came to Atlanta the next day?"

"Yes, but I didn't see her that weekend. I talked to her a couple of times on the phone, but she wouldn't see me. I even tried going out to Tech and trying to surprise her. That didn't work either. So the last time I talked to her I gave her the number at the hotel, and told her to call me if I could help her."

"Where were you Monday evening, the night she was killed?"

"At the hotel," Eddie said. "You see, if she was really in danger, I wanted to be there to get the call. I got so I didn't want to stay out any time at all. I kept thinking she'd call and need my help, and I might be out."

"If this is true, you ought to turn yourself in."

"No. I killed that policeman behind the hotel. I can't change that."

"You kill anybody else?" I asked. "A little black guy named Ferd?"

"No," he said. "Who's he?"

"Just another killing."

"The policeman was more killing than I wanted."

We were driving out past all those god-awful apartment complexes with their nine-hole golf courses and man-made lakes. Eddie wasn't watching the scenery at all. He watched me and the road ahead.

"Why are you still in town?"

"I don't care if I die doing it, but I'm going to kill whoever killed Emily."

"We might never find out who did it. You know how many unsolved murders there are every year in Atlanta?"

"I've heard about you, Hardman. You can find out."

"I'm not working for you. If I find him, the police get him."

"I couldn't hire you, anyway. I don't have any money." He pointed toward a cutoff we were approaching. "Turn around and head back to town."

I got into the lane and got turned around. The traffic was light. I guess everybody was at home, enjoying their central heating. It was where I thought I ought to be. The temperature was dropping pretty fast, and it was going to be a bitchy night out when the sun went down.

"Give it up, Eddie. You don't have a chance."

"No." His lips were trembling, but the .45 on his thigh was steady. "They're going to have to kill me. I mean it."

Maybe I should have done something tricky and had a try at taking him. Maybe. But I'd seen the holes in the cop behind the hotel, and I didn't think of myself as suicidal. I drove back to town and we didn't talk much. When we reached Baker and Peachtree he told me to pull over, and I did. He tucked the .45 into the raincoat pocket but it was still pointed at me.

"Find him for me, Hardman."

"I'll try."

"You see, I loved Emily, and I can't stand to have people thinking I killed her. I wouldn't have done that … not in a thousand years." He pushed the door open. "Drive straight on. Don't turn or stop." He was out of the car in one quick movement and on the curb, watching me. He slammed the door and I drove on. I looked back once and saw him still there, watching me. Then he set out at a fast walk in the opposite direction. I lost sight of him, and I knew it wouldn't do any good to turn around and circle the block. He'd be gone by then.

He'd probably pick up a cab at the Regency or one cruising. And, to tell the truth, I had mixed feelings about Eddie. I didn't like the killing of the cop, but I could understand how he felt about Emily … if he was telling the truth. I wanted him caught, but I didn't want it badly enough to do it myself. On the drive home, I went over what he'd said and how he'd said it, and I started believing him. He'd killed the cop, but he hadn't killed Emily or Ferd. Now Hump and I could make another list, and it would be a leaner one. And we'd look around in the life of Emily Campbell, to see what she knew that could get her killed.

It wasn't until I'd called three French restaurants for reservations and got no answer to my calls that I realized that the good restaurants weren't open on Sunday. Atlanta's a blue-law city, and I guess without the wine and the drinks, it's just not worth the trouble to open the doors. When I called Marcy, she said the French restaurant could wait. She'd fix some kind of supper for me.

I went over around eight and began my courtship.

Hump went along when I dropped by to see The Man the next morning. A cold gray rain that was almost ice fell around us with the rustle of a glass bead curtain. It rattled on the windshield and plinked on the roof. It wasn't a day for walking, so I said screw it and went around the block near The Man's place a time or two, while Hump watched to see if we had any interested followers. He didn't think so, and I broke off the second circle tight and parked in the lot next to the building where The Man's apartment was. As a last thought, because it might cause trouble, I shucked my .38 and left it in the glove box. Hump grinned and said he wasn't carrying any today because he knew I'd protect him.

The black with the pump gun met us at the bottom of the stairs and followed us up the flight with the pump gun over his shoulder. "He'll be out in a minute," he said when we were in the apartment. Without another look at us, he sat in the chair facing the door, with the pump gun across his knees.

The Man came out of the bedroom about ten minutes later. He was wearing one of those bright yellow mod jump suits with matching cloth shoes and a kelly green scarf around his neck. "Coffee, gentlemen, before we talk?"

It was time to push the crap aside. "We want to talk to you alone."

"I'm alone." His mouth thinned and hardened. He didn't like the way I'd talked to him. He wasn't used to it.

"Without him." I nodded at the black with the pump gun.

The black with the pump gun moved his head slowly and showed me his rock-hard eyes. He didn't move the pump gun, but it was in his face that he could and he would.

"I don't know if I trust you that much, Hardman."

"It's late in the day for that," I said. "If I was a headhunter I'd already have yours."

Hump saw the standoff balance still there and he stepped into it. "Hardman's straight. It's shit-or-get-off-the-pot time."

The Man looked up at Hump. He didn't like looking up at anybody, and his face showed it. "You've been turning white for a long time, Hump. You get a shade whiter every day."

Hump's voice was a cold whisper. "Talk one more string of shit like that to me, and I'm going to teach you country manners." He was talking to The Man but when he moved, his quickness almost a blur, it was toward the black with the shotgun. When he stopped, he was a step away from the black, and the gun hadn't moved from its position. The black was stunned, and he gave up on it. He might get a round off, but it would end up in the wall across from us. If he'd been larger and stronger, he'd have tried to use the butt, swinging it upward and away from his hip. The massiveness of Hump told him that that wouldn't work either.

It was still a kind of standoff, but Hump had swung the balance. The Man looked at the black and said, "Wait out on the steps." The Man didn't like being beaten. It was going to be a long day for the black after we left.

The black eased out of the chair, not making a sudden movement. When he was halfway up, a little off balance, Hump reached out and jerked the pump gun from his hands.

"You can leave this," Hump said.

The black went outside and closed the door behind him. Hump placed the pump gun on the bar counter, muzzle away from us. He stepped away from it, showing that it wasn't a factor any more.

The Man took all this in before he eased himself down on the sofa. "I don't approve of your methods, but talk if you want to."

"I saw the kid, Eddie Spence, yesterday. He said he didn't kill Emily and he didn't kill Ferd."

"You believe him?"

"Close to it," I said. "He admits killing the cop. I don't see why he'd lie about the other two. Three killings don't make you any deader than one, especially if that one is a cop."

"Does he know about me?" The Man asked.

"I don't think so. The poor dumb sonofabitch is just running around in circles. He doesn't know where he's going. He's waiting for somebody to find Emily's killer so he can take a crack at him."

The Man nodded. He seemed to relax. "Then who killed Emily and Ferd?"

"That's my question," I said. I looked at Hump.

Hump stepped in smoothly "We thought you might know."

"I didn't kill them."

"You might know who did," Hump said.

"Without knowing you know," I added.

"If I knew..." The Man broke off and shook his head.

It was my turn again. "Three nights before she died, Emily called Eddie Spence at a pool hall in Millhouse. She was afraid. She said she'd found out something that could get her killed."

Amazement showed on The Man's face. "Why didn't she come to me? I would have protected her. She knew that."

"Maybe the thing that could get her killed she got from you. That meant you were blocked out. She couldn't come to you without letting you know that she knew something she wasn't supposed to know."

He wouldn't accept that. "We didn't do that kind of pillow talk."

"It didn't have to be something you told her. It could have been something she found out by accident."

His eyes were closed and he was trying to think. Frustration was all across his face. The idea was too new for him, and he was drawing a blank. "It doesn't make sense. I always kept her away on nights when I had business here. I always made a check through the apartment when she was coming over, to make sure I'd left nothing out of the safe."

"Shit, get off it," I said angrily. "It has to be something from over here. Say she's got three parts to her life: home, Tech and here. Her family hasn't seen her in a long time and it's not likely they'd kill her, right? At Tech, who's going to kill her? Betty Lou down the hall, because Emily knows that Betty Lou blew a basketball player? That's silly. But over here, this is where the dirty money is, the big dirty money. People kill for it over here. It's a fact of this kind of life. And think about Ferd. Maybe Ferd knew what Emily knew. He might have been slow in the head, but he might have figured it out. Maybe that's why somebody killed him."

"There are a lot of maybes in that," The Man said. "I'll have to think on it. It might come to me."

"And you'll call me when it does?" I nodded at Hump and we started out.

"I will," The Man said.

With his hand on the door, Hump turned back to him. "We still working for you? It might be good to know."

The Man jerked his head a couple of times. He hadn't liked us before and now he liked us even less. But he still had a use for us.

On the steps, going in, the black passed us without a word.

I drove through the cold rain back to Hump's apartment. The traffic was slow and cautious. "The Man doesn't like us any more," I said.

"He'll get over it, given time. But that poor black stud with the shotgun won't … ever. He'll be headed north with a bus ticket before the afternoon's over. He saw The Man lose some face, and he won't be around to talk about it."

"You think The Man told us all he knew?"

Hump nodded. "The surprise had him good. If he knew, it would have slipped out. Now he's going to worry his head sore."

"And when he figures it out?"

"He won't call us. He'll handle it himself."

I believed that, too. It was what I'd been afraid of. It was a risk, a chance I'd taken. But he hadn't come up with a name, and it had slipped out of my hands. There was no way of knowing how bloody it would get before it was all over.

I stopped by Hump's long enough to pack up the gear I'd left at his apartment. Now that I knew Eddie Spence wasn't gunning for me, there wasn't any reason to impose on him any longer. I had the feeling I'd been getting in the way of his happy love life. On the way home, I stopped by Cloudt's and stocked up on groceries and meat. At a nearby wine shop I got a couple of cases of beer and a bottle of Chateau Latour '53 that I'd been eying for a month or so. It was too damned expensive, but it was supposed to be a good year, and I'd bought a couple of beautiful steaks. It was time to ask Marcy over to cook for me. The Chateau Latour '53 was just the kind of extra that might make the whole evening. Anyway, it was only money.

"I don't think I know you well enough to cook and sew for you," Marcy said when I finally reached her.

I said I was sorry she felt that way. I was so tired after all the shopping and cleaning that I couldn't stand high-life dining. Still, I could understand her point of view, and I hoped she'd see mine. I wasn't about to waste those two steaks or the bottle of Latour '53.

"Chateau Latour 1953? Wait while I look that up in my wine book."

"Too late," I said. "I'll call the go-go dancer. She's kind of ugly, but she cooks well."

Marcy said I could pick her up around six-thirty. And she wanted to hear a bit more about my friend, the go-go dancer.

On the way to pick up Marcy, I stopped off to see Art. Edna let me in and said that Art was in the bathroom, shaving. "Go on in."

"That was some blind date you fixed me up with," I said.

"Like her, did you?"

"Not as bad as most of the blind dates I get."

I left her in the center of the living room, smiling, and went through the bedroom and stopped in the bathroom doorway.

"Anything new?" I asked.

"Nothing."

"You're not going to like this ..."

The razor stopped in mid-stroke. "You talked to Eddie Spence?"

While he finished shaving, I told him about the meeting and what had been said. I added the dyed hair and the mustache and the blue raincoat and the tweed jacket.

He came up blubbering from the face rinse in the sink. "You wait a whole day. Why tell me now? Why not wait until you write your memoirs?"

"You catch the right man and you're going to have the makings of a Ruby-Oswald on your hands. Don't say you weren't warned."

"Okay, I'm warned."

"I'm not after Eddie any more. That's your job."

"Now you can tell me who you're really working for," Art said.

"The twenty thousand dollar reward."

"Changed clients, huh?"

"I've got a question." I lit a cigarette and reached past Art to drop the match in the john. "Where was Ben Coleman when Emily Campbell got killed?"

"Coleman?"

"Campbell's business manager," I said.

"Oh, him. He was with Campbell all evening at the Regency. They were going over some investments."

I blew smoke at the ceiling. "Anybody else with them?"

"No."

"Any waiters bringing up coffee or booze, and at what time?"

"We didn't check." Art pushed past me and into the bedroom. "You know anything I don't about Coleman?"

"No, but I'd appreciate it if you'd have this checked out. Might as well touch all the bases."

"As long as you don't have to do the legwork," Art said.

"I don't have time," I said. "Have to pick up Marcy." I got away while he was struggling into a t-shirt.

The try for me, when it came, almost worked.

The evening and the courtship had gone well. Marcy had tossed a salad of green peppers, lettuce and artichoke hearts, and we'd had that with the steaks and the wine. The wine was like they said it'd be, and I decided that if I got a part of the twenty thousand dollars, I was going to buy a couple of cases of it. After dinner, with the coffee, I broke out a bottle of five-star Metaxa I'd been saving for an occasion.

Around midnight, I left my place to drive Marcy home. I was feeling a little foolish, like the courtship had made me around sixteen years old, going back to when I didn't know the facts. But it was a good foolish, and I knew that if we ever grew up, we'd be the better for it. During the drive, Marcy opened the glove box while looking for a Kleenex. She found the tissue, but she also found my .38 where I'd put it that morning, when Hump and I had gone to see The Man.

"I didn't know you still played with guns, Jim."

"Sometimes."

"I never liked guns."

"I usually keep it in the house." At a light, after she had a tissue, I reached across her and closed the glove box.

But I remembered the gun later when I was back at home, getting out of the car in the driveway. I leaned back across the seat, punched open the glove box and got it out. I was stepping from the driveway to the walkway, just rounding the corner hedges, when I noticed two things that seemed wrong. The light over the front steps was off, and I remembered that I'd switched it on so Marcy wouldn't twist an ankle. Of course, that could mean that the bulb had burned out. But at the same time, I heard a faint rustle in the leaves near the far hedge ahead of me, the one that separated my house from the next one. Of course, that could be some small animal like a cat, or the wind. The two together didn't add up right. Quickly, knowing I'd feel like an idiot if nothing happened, I made a belly-dive for the bushes at the side of the house. A shotgun blasted at me, at where I'd been only a second before. I heard the pellets strike the side of the house and, after my ears got over the blast, I heard the footsteps heading for the road. I pushed away from the bushes and got to one knee. The .38 was still in my hand and I swung it up in a reflex movement that brought my left hand across to grip my right wrist and steady my aim. When I saw the dark shape running parallel to the hedge row, I got off three shots as fast as I could. The wind grunted out of him, and the shotgun pitched into the street gutter with a clatter. When I got to him he was hanging in the hedge, thrown there by the impact. I pulled him away and stretched him out on the lawn. And then I got my surprise. All the time after I'd fired, during the slow, careful walk toward him, I was sure it would be the black from The Man's apartment, the one that Hump and I had humbled earlier in the day.

It wasn't that man at all. It was a short, stocky white man who looked to be in his forties. He was wearing an Army fatigue jacket and, under that, matching green twill work shirt and pants, and heavy black work shoes. I'd never seen him before. As I looked down at him, seeing the dark blood spill from a chest wound, he gurgled and died.

CHAPTER THIRTEEN

"His name was Fred Mullidge."

We were in Art's office at the department. The shotgun was on the edge of the desk, between us. It was battered and scarred, like it had been through a number of hunting seasons. But it was well cared for and I couldn't see any signs of rust. I looked down at the stock and saw the "F.M." scratched there.

"No identification on the body. A car down the road, a '55 Chevy, was registered to Mullidge, and the prints matched up with the ones in our records." Art stopped and looked at me. "You know him?"

"No."

"If you don't know him, why was he trying to kill you?"

"Beyond me."

"You expect me to believe that?" Art said. "A man tries to kill you, and you don't know him?"

I nodded.

"You working on anything besides the Campbell girl's death?"

"No."

"You sure?" Art looked hard and mean as hell. Friendship was one thing, but a new death was something else.

"Art, I swear."

"You messing around with any women in his family? His wife? His daughter?"

"Not unless Marcy is his wife or his daughter."

"Goddamn it, Hardman. It was a cold night out there, and he wasn't standing around in your front yard for no reason at all."

"He was there for a reason," I said. "He was there to kill me, and he went to the trouble of unscrewing the front porch light. He gave my house two barrels. But I still don't know him." I grinned at Art. "You think my mortgage insurance covers shotgun wounds the house receives when people shoot at me?"

"Only if they hit you," Art said sourly.

"What else you have on Mullidge?"

"Army in the Korean. Did a tour there. Honorable discharge. Worked in a cigarette factory in Durham, North Carolina. Drifted down here in 1960 of so. A number of nothing jobs. Last listed job was with a big parking lot over by the Capitol. Since then, he's been working through those day-by-day temporary labor contractors down around Whitehall. Also sold his blood now and then. Arrested two times for drunk and disorderly, one for driving under the influence, and one for assault." Art looked up at me and shook his head. "Not with a gun. Hit somebody with a beer bottle, at one of the skid-row beer places."

"Then somebody bought themselves some cheap labor."

"Who wants you dead?"

"Not Eddie Spence. It must be somebody else."

Art lit a cigarette and blew the smoke across the desk at me. "You messing in the rackets now?"

"This look like a racket try to you?" The question jolted me for a second. I began to wonder if he knew about the trips that Hump and I took to New York now and then. "If he was a racket hit man, I'd be in the morgue getting a chill now, instead of him."

"So ...?"

"I'll do some legwork in the morning. Give me the names of the labor contractors and the parking lot he worked for. I'll spend some time trying to find out who Fred Mullidge knew that I know."

Art scribbled on a memo pad and passed the pad to me. *25 Hour Labor Force. Quik Labor. Capitol Parking Lot.* I tore off the sheet and put it in my pocket.

"Can I go now?"

Art nodded. "Let me know what you find out."

I said I would. When I got home I started to call Marcy, but I realized that the shooting wouldn't be in the morning paper. I'd let her sleep and call her in the morning, before she left for work, before she could hear it on the radio.

All night long, alone in my double bed, I thought about the blood drying on the front lawn leaves. I'd killed before, but it never got easy. And then, toward morning light, it began to rain. I slept for a time, knowing the rain was washing the blood away from the lawn, down into the earth or into the storm gutters. I liked to think that it washed all the way down to the sea, but I knew that really wasn't possible.

At seven-thirty the alarm went off. I got up and put on the water for the coffee. When it boiled, I made a cup of instant and dialed Hump's number. He sounded grumpy for a few seconds, and then he said that I was one lucky white man. I agreed, and said for him to get himself together and I'd call him back later. We'd be making the rounds of the labor contractors.

"Marcy know yet?" Hump asked.

"I'm going to call her now."

He hung up and I called Marcy. She sounded sleepy and warm, like she hadn't been awake long. I tried to make a bit of small talk, but it didn't come off well. So I went ahead and told her about the hit try, without any frills on it. Maybe I was too blunt, because I heard her suck in her breath.

"I'll be right over," she said.

"I'm not hurt."

Marcy hung up on me.

Twenty minutes later, we were standing in my living room, me holding her while she shook and shivered. She was crying, too, and I could hear, almost under her breath, "You … you … sonofabitch … if you … if you think… I spent … a good year … almost two years … getting … ready for you … and you're … you're going to … get killed … on me … then you've got … another thing coming."

Holding her, I was looking at her face. She wasn't wearing make-up, and I could see the milk blue veins in her eyelids and the crinkly tracks of wrinkles in the corners of her eyes. I tried to remember why I always thought of her as twenty-five, when she was probably thirty. There were fat drops of rain in her hair, and I suddenly felt a massive tenderness for her.

"This is some fucking courtship," I said.

In time she stopped shivering and we were warm together, and I could feel the slight bony push of her pelvis.

We spent the rest of the morning in bed. Making love part of the time, and the rest of the time talking. Talking was easier without clothes, and she told me how she'd plotted the whole year and how she hadn't been with a man the whole time.

"A waste," I said.

"Think of it as a savings account, instead," she said.

And, late in the morning, the rain changed to sleet, and we slept for a time, listening to the dry, brittle clack of rain on the bedroom window.

I'd called Hump after Marcy came by and told him the morning had been called because of rain. At twelve-thirty, I called him and told him it was on again. Marcy wanted to wait for me at my place, but I didn't like the idea of leaving her there alone. There might be another try. I saw her off a few minutes before Hump drove up.

The sign in the window of the *25 Hour Labor Force* read "Needed 105 Men" but the battered school desks held only dozing winos, and nobody seemed to be paying much attention to them. If they needed 105 men, it must have been much earlier in the day, or on some other day.

"I'm afraid that's information I can't give out." The desk plaque gave his name as John C. Armour, Manager. He looked like he had dirt in the long creases of his face. His tie had been washed along with his underwear, and the tie's small knot held together a white shirt that wasn't white any more.

I dropped the early edition of *The Journal,* the afternoon paper, on his desk. One of the lead stories was about the death of Fred Mullidge, and I'd marked it with a thick black line. "That won't cut it," I said. "I was the one he was shooting at."

"Oh, that Fred Mullidge." He folded the paper and handed it back to me. "He did work through our company now and then."

"I'd like to see his file."

"That's not possible." But his face changed, and I knew why. Hump had shifted his feet and moved forward. I didn't need to look at him. I knew that he looked mean and irritated, like he'd beat your ass for a nickel. So that set the pattern: I'd be reasonable and Hump would be near violence, and we'd catch Armour in the whipsaw. "The files are private," Armour protested, but it was like a gasp.

"He's dead now," I said, "and that's about as public as you can get."

Armour wasn't listening to me. He was looking past me, at Hump. "He didn't work for us that much." He turned in his swivel chair and rode it two or three feet to a file cabinet. "We kept files only when the person had some special job skill. That way, if he didn't come by one day and we needed him, we could call him." He pulled out one file drawer and walked his fingers over up to the "M" section. He took out a file and crabbed back to the desk. "In the case of Mullidge, he had some experience in trucking."

When he opened the file I got out my pad and uncapped my pen. "Address?"

He gave me a number on Ponce De Leon. "I think that's the last one he gave us. I think it's a boarding house."

"Did he give references?"

"We don't usually need those. He did give us a partial listing." He read off the tobacco company in Durham. "Drove a truck for them." He ran his finger down the single sheet of paper. "Worked in a parking lot, but I don't have the name of it. Also did custodial work for the state. That is, he was a janitor."

"He say where he worked?"

"I think it was one of the buildings over by the State Capitol." Armour closed the file. "That's all I have."

"No record of jobs he worked on for you?"

"That's too much bookkeeping."

On the way out, we passed the still-dozing winos, and the sign still said they needed 105 men.

The *Quik Labor* office didn't add anything new. They had the same list of previous jobs and the same Ponce De Leon address. On the way out, I happened to look back and saw the manager dropping Mullidge's file into the trash can. It seemed final somehow, like a funeral.

The Capitol Parking Lot is on Central, almost in the shadow of the state buildings. There's room for forty or so cars, and there's a cramped booth where the attendant sits next to a small electric heater in the fall and winter. The attendant was a young black who didn't look more than sixteen. I turned the car over to him and watched him whip it into a narrow space that I'd have passed up.

"You try him," I said to Hump, as the black kid walked back toward us. I walked away a few steps and lit a cigarette. They talked for a few minutes, with the kid cutting his eyes toward me a time or two. Hump patted him on the shoulder and came over to me.

"The owner's a guy named George Herndon, and he's due in an hour or so. The kid doesn't know Mullidge but he's heard about him. Herndon uses Mullidge in his pitch for honesty. It seems that Mullidge had a tendency toward a bit of stealing."

"I'd like to hear Herndon's sermon."

Hump looked in both directions. "It's lunchtime."

We found a small diner and ordered. I got a dime from Hump and went back to the phone booth. Hugh Muffin answered on the second ring. "Hardman, I've been reading about you in the afternoon paper."

"Lies," I said.

"You been walking around in that fellow's flower garden?"

"I never met his wife, if he had one."

"Why was he after you?" Hugh asked.

"Maybe you can help me." I gave him the information I had about Mullidge working for the state as a janitor, and asked if he'd find out where Mullidge had worked. I gave him the pay phone's number and went back to the booth where Hump was. I was halfway through a tough hot roast beef sandwich when the phone rang. I beat the waiter to it by a step.

"Mullidge worked for the state for about six months. Quit around a year and a half ago. The girl I talked to said there was a note in his file that he wasn't to be hired again. Something to do with some missing items in the offices he was cleaning. Nothing definite, but the stealing stopped as soon as he was gone."

"Where'd he work?"

"In my building," Hugh said.

"You know him?"

"Not that I know of. Of course, there are a lot of them on the cleaning detail, and most of it is done at night or early in the morning, when we're not here."

"Thanks, Hugh."

"You think this is tied to the Campbell case?"

"I don't know, but it's the only case I'm on right now."

"Maybe it was a mistake," Hugh said.

"It was for Mullidge."

When the hour was up, we walked back toward the Capitol Parking Lot.

"That Hugh," Hump said, "has got as many crooked sides as four snakes fucking."

"Why?"

"Just a feeling I get around him. Like he's got eight faces, and he can show you any of them with a split second's warning."

"He's a political animal. He's been at it a long time, so long he probably doesn't know which one is the real one. If there's a real one left."

"Funny about Mullidge working in his building at one time, wasn't it?"

"There must be five hundred offices in that building," I said.

"The only one you know there is old Hugh."

"No," I said, "I know Arch Campbell, too."

It was odd, but just that—nothing else that I could see. I couldn't think of any connection between Mullidge and Hugh, or between Mullidge and Arch Campbell. I worried it around for a time, and then I let it drop. It didn't make much sense that I could see, and the more I worried it around, the less it made.

The black kid got the car out of the tight place without losing a flake of paint. Hump sat in it and waited while I talked to Herndon. George Herndon was short and potbellied, and was like a lot of the rednecks you'd see on any weekend afternoon, out at the Braves games. He chewed tobacco and, when he talked, I could see the brown-black tongue worry the cud about.

"Fred Mullidge don't work here anymore."

"He's dead," I said.

"That a fact?" He stopped the cud. "How?"

"Shot, early this morning."

He turned away from me deliberately and spat a dark stream toward the gutter. "I knew he'd come to no good."

"How long he work for you?"

"Oh, four months, more or less. Seemed hard-working enough. Never late opening that I could tell. But I started getting complaints."

"Things missing out of the cars?"

"How'd you know?"

"It's common knowledge," I said. "What was he stealing?"

The shrewd eyes mocked me. "That's not common knowledge, too?"

I laughed. "You got me there."

"I thought so." Herndon grinned at me. "It was just some tapes for those car tape players, at first. At least, I got some complaints that some were missing. I didn't think much of it, at first. But when I got more and more complaints, I took a look in the trunk of Mullidge's old car while he was at lunch one day. I found a whole cardboard box of stolen plunder in there."

"Didn't sound too bright, having the stuff right on the premises."

"He was bright enough," Herndon said. "He had pull of some kind, because he should have gone to jail for a year. Somebody must have fixed it, because he never served a day."

"You know who fixed it?"

He spat again. "It's just a guess. All I know is, he never served a day."

The boarding house was one of those high, wood-frame houses set far back on the lot from the street, with a steep lawn in front.

From the main entrance, when the storm door was open, the rank scent of turnip greens blew past me. Along with it, came the dry, dusty blast of air from the heating system.

"Yes, I read about it in the afternoon paper, and I've been expecting the police ever since." Mrs. Burleson was around fifty, a hulk of a woman, with a greasy blue dress and a gravy-stained apron. Over the dress and the apron, she wore a man's brown sweater that the moths must have been eating at over the last few summers.

"Did you call them?" I asked.

"Why should I? Me call them?"

"He wasn't carrying any identification. They don't know where he lived."

"Is that right?"

I could see the gears begin to move slowly. I got out my wallet and handed her a five. "I'd like to look around his room."

"Oh, I couldn't let you do that."

"The police'll be over later." I added another five. "I can call them now, but they won't pay you ten for a look."

"It's still not right."

I put out my hand. Mrs. Burleson jerked the money away and stuffed it down the front of her dress. "He was behind in his rent, anyway." She dug a key from the apron pocket. "It's on the second floor, the third door on the left."

It was a neat room. That surprised me. The bed was made, and a couple of cheap Army surplus blankets were smoothed and stretched across it. A pair of low-cut black shoos, polished to a high gloss and stretched on shoe trees, were under the front edge of the bed. In the shallow, dark closet, I found a gray suit with a shiny seat to the trousers, two Robert Hall sport coats, one for winter and one for spring, and, four or five pairs of slacks. In the low, three-drawer dresser were the twins to the green twill work clothes Mullidge had died in, as well as shirts and underwear neatly folded and stacked and half a dozen pairs of white cotton socks.

Still no wallet. I looked around the room. I went to the bed and pushed the pillow aside. Not there. But, lifting the pillow to replace it, I felt the lump inside. I shook the pillow, and the wallet fell onto the tight blankets and bounced back at me.

It was an old leather wallet, sweat-darkened on the curved side that fitted his hip, cracking with dry rot along the edges. In the money compartment a ten and three ones. No blood money yet. I pulled out the mass of cards and yellowing scraps of paper, and found it in there: four fifty-dollar bills, folded and creased sharply so they wouldn't bulk.

So that was what I was worth dead: two hundred dollars.

I jammed the cards, the scraps of paper and the money back into the wallet and dropped it into my topcoat pocket. Another walk around the room revealed nothing else worth noting. It was the room of a compulsively neat person. Taught by his mother to wash behind his ears, and taught by the Army to make a tight bed, shine his shoes, and keep his clothes ready for inspection. He'd been neat everywhere but in my front yard.

Hump was in the car drinking Crystal Shop coffee from a place a couple of blocks away. He handed me a cup. "Find anything?"

"The fee was two hundred dollars."

"That's cheap, for bloodletting."

"Buy cheap, and you get shoddy work," I said.

"It wasn't that shoddy."

Edna cleared away Art's supper dishes and brought in coffee cups for Hump and me. She put a fresh pot of coffee on the table and stopped in the doorway, ready to go into another part of the house. "Mr. Evans, the boys are going to be sorry they weren't here to meet you."

"Tell them to call me and I'll drop by sometime," Hump said.

"I will," Edna said.

After she left, Art took the wallet and dumped the contents on the table. He put the four fifties aside. "You're coming up in the world, Jim. When you were a cop, your life was worth about a ten-cent candy bar."

"Or a nickel roll of Lifesavers." It was true enough. In my time on the force, I'd seen policemen killed for a lot less.

We spent a few minutes going through the wad of paper scraps. We ended up with three piles. In one pile we put the ones with girls' names and phone numbers. In another we separated the scraps with men's names, with or without phone numbers. In the final pile we put the ones that had only phone numbers, no names and addresses.

"We'll check a couple of the women, but I doubt that there's anything there. I'll start a check on the others as soon as I get to the office."

"One thing more, Art," I said.

"Yeah?" Art was putting the paper scraps from the wallet into envelopes.

"A little over a year ago, Mullidge was arrested for stealing from the cars at the parking lot where he worked. The owner thinks it was fixed, that Mullidge must have had some kind of clout higher up."

Art made a note. "I'll ask around"

"Maybe it's somebody I know."

Art put the pad in his shirt pocket. "Speaking of asking around for you, Ben Coleman was with Arch Campbell the night Emily was killed. They were in Arch's room at the Regency, going over some investment plans. Room service took them ice and mixers around eight, and a pot of coffee a bit after eleven. The same hotel man took up both orders. One of my men showed him Coleman's photo. He swears that Coleman was in the room both times he took stuff in."

"The three hours and a bit between, that's a lot of time," Hump said.

"More than enough to go out, find and kill Emily, and make it back to Campbell's room for coffee," I said.

"Give me a reason Coleman'd kill Emily," Art said.

"I don't have one at the moment," I admitted. "But he's a pretty shifty guy."

"And give me one reason why Campbell would cover for Coleman while he was out killing Campbell's daughter."

"When you put it that way," I said, "it does sound silly, doesn't it?"

Art nodded. "It makes you sound senile."

"I don't think so. Something's not right with him. Hump was with me when I asked him how well he knew Emily."

Hump nodded. "He got uptight. Blew up."

"Just because Coleman might have had a thing for Emily ... if he did ... that doesn't mean he'd kill her," Art said.

"That's funny." I turned and winked at Hump.

"What's funny?"

"Having a thing for Emily. That's exactly why you think Eddie Spence killed her."

"Oh, shit."

The phone was ringing when I got home, a bit after midnight. On the way back from Marcy's, I'd stopped off to borrow Hump's shotgun and part of a box of shells. I put the shotgun on the sofa and made a run for the bedroom. I probably got it on the last ring.

"Hardman?" It was The Man.

"Yes."

"I've been trying to reach you all day, ever since I read the *Journal*"

"I've been out most of the day, trying to find out who wants me dead."

"Find anything?"

"So far, it's dark and muddy."

"I just thought I'd let you know that I didn't send the gun after you," The Man said.

"I figured as much. The day you send out cheap white labor, then I'll be sure you're slipping."

"Of course, sending out a white ass after you, that would be a good smokescreen."

"Only," I said, "if you planned on him missing me and getting killed."

"That's true." The Man laughed.

"You been doing any thinking?"

"About what?" The laugh died and he sounded withdrawn, as if he'd moved the receiver away from his mouth.

"About what Emily might have known that she wasn't supposed to."

"Nothing yet." But he still sounded far away.

"Keep trying."

He said he would, and then he lied and said he'd call me as soon as he had something. I pretended to believe him and said good-bye and hung up on him.

I slept that night with Hump's shotgun on the bed beside me. At first it reassured me. But, during the night, I rolled over and found myself touching it several times. Near morning, when there was light beyond the drawn shades, I got up and put the shotgun on a chair at the foot of the bed. Maybe that turned the trick. I dropped off into a deep sleep that I thought I'd never come out of.

CHAPTER FOURTEEN

I woke up the next morning to a ringing that I thought was the telephone. I got the receiver to my ear but the line was dead. But the ringing was still going on, so it had to be the doorbell. By the time I had that figured out, the doorbell had stopped and somebody was hammering on the door frame. It sounded like they were using the root end of a tree stump. From the angle of the winter sun, it was late morning. I didn't feel too rested. I guess that was the result of sleeping part of the night with the shotgun. It made for an uneasy night, like sleeping with a girl you didn't like or trust.

I stumbled through the living room and got the front door open. Hump stood there, shivering, with his topcoat collar up. I waved him in and headed for the kitchen.

"I guess you haven't been listening to the radio," he said behind me.

"Not yet. Why?" I lit the gas under the kettle of water and went to the refrigerator for a glass of juice.

"The police think they've got Eddie Spence bottled up in Piedmont Park."

I took a swallow of orange juice from the pitcher and went over and whirled the dial on the kitchen radio. I went past four or five rock-and-roll stations and one prayer meeting of the air before I found the news. "...and Georgia Tech co-ed, Emily Campbell. A suspect matching Spence's description robbed the Georgia People's Trust at Eighteenth and Peachtree of an undetermined amount. A witness at the scene said the suspect drove away in a Yellow cab that had been parked in front of the bank. A few minutes later, the cab was found abandoned near the Fourteenth Street entrance to Piedmont Park. Police have closed off all entrances and exits and ..."

I got down two cups and spooned in instant coffee. "When I talked to him Sunday, he said he was short of cash."

Hump slumped down into one of the kitchen chairs. "The abandoned cab thing, what does that mean to you?"

"He's too smart to get caught that way. The police'll find two or three dope dealers and a couple of hippies having their noon fuck in a sleeping bag." I poured the boiling water into the cups and passed the sugar and milk to Hump.

"... the cab driver, Edwin Benson of Northeast Atlanta, was found bound and gagged in a wooded lot near Piedmont and Monroe. He said a young white male hailed him near the corner of Tenth and Peachtree ..."

I nodded at Hump. "That's it. He's got another car. He parks his car somewhere around Thirteenth or Fourteenth, between Piedmont and Peachtree. He walks over to Tenth and hails a cab, shows the cabbie the .45, and has him drive to the wooded lot. Then, maybe even wearing the cab driver's hat, he drives to the bank, robs it, and drives away. Goes the four or five blocks and leaves the cab. A short walk to his car, and off he goes. My guess is that he's nowhere near the Park right now."

"The cops that dumb?"

"I bet they've made the same guess. Policemen are knocking on doors all around that area to see it they can find somebody who saw Spence get into another car. At the same time, the Park's nearby, and they've got to cover that as a possibility."

Hump grinned. "I guess I got you up for nothing."

"It was time, anyway." I made breakfast and Hump had a second cup of coffee. An hour later, a news report said the police had finished their sweep through the Park. There'd been no sign of Eddie Spence. The search had, however, uncovered a cache of grass and two bottles of pills thought to be illegal drugs.

The phone rang a few minutes after Hump left. By the kitchen clock, it was twelve-thirty-five.

"Mr. Hardman?"

"Yes."

"Ben Coleman here. I thought you'd be out at Piedmont Park."

"That's a fool's errand," I said.

"Meaning…?"

"Eddie Spence wasn't anywhere near that search going on in the Park. I'd have been warmer looking in my own backyard."

"I see," Coleman said. "Oh, I was sorry to hear about the attempt on your life. I understand it was a close thing."

"It was close," I said.

"Well, keep in touch. Mr. Campbell is interested in any progress you make."

I said I would, and I knew Mr. Campbell was, and then I rang off. It was a nonsense call, and I couldn't see why Coleman had gone to the trouble. Of course, I hadn't been too friendly to him. There was always the chance that he'd called for some good reason and had been put off by me. Someday I was just going to have to get around to being a little more pleasant to people.

Around five, I drove over to Art's house. I found him in the backyard, raking leaves. He'd already filled three leaf bags and was working on his fourth. "It gets later every year," he said. "I used to do this in October or November, and here it is almost Christmas."

"Edna got on your back, huh?"

"She's been on it for a month. It seems the neighbors don't like our leaves blowing over onto their lawns."

"An act of God," I said.

"The neighbors don't believe that much in God."

I held the mouth of the bag open while Art scooped the leaves in with his hands. "Anything yet on the Mullidge numbers and addresses?"

"Not yet," Art said. "He seems to have been a pack rat for that kind of thing. I had a couple of men checking that out last night. Some of the addresses and numbers go way back. So far, we've found two girls he met in bars, but they didn't know him well."

"How about the pressure that got him off without doing time?"

"That's a hard one. People don't like to admit they were paid off or exchanged favors. I'm going to have to be sly with that one."

I agreed that was probably best. Art put the rake in the garage, and we carried the leaf bags out to the street. We stacked them there for the garbage trucks.

"Stay to supper," Art said.

"Can't, but I'd like to use your phone."

While Art washed up, I called Marcy.

"It's about time you called, Jim. I thought you'd taken my virtue and decided to forget about me." She sounded warm and a little amused.

"I was," I said, "but the ugly go-go dancer had to work tonight."

"You're a hard man."

"I thought we might boil up a few pounds of shrimp."

"My place or yours?" Marcy asked.

"Mine. I wouldn't want to hurt your reputation."

When she finished jeering at me, I said I'd pick her up in thirty or forty-five minutes, after I'd done my shopping.

The fish store was closed. I had to beat on the door before they'd open up for me. I bought four pounds of shrimp and paid the employee a dollar extra, so he wouldn't mind working overtime. On the way out to Marcy's, I stopped at a beer and wine store and bought two six-packs of Beck's beer and a bottle of Inglenook Chablis.

When the water was boiling, I threw in a whole peeled onion, a handful of celery tops and a couple of bay leaves. I turned the gas low so it would simmer, and went back over to the sink to help Marcy finish the peeling and deveining. It took a lot longer than I thought it would, and we were on our second Beck's when we finished the last of the shrimp. With the shells gone, four pounds didn't seem like very much. Marcy cleaned up the sink while I dumped the shrimp into the pot and stood over them, waiting for the first moment they turn pink. At that instant I cut the gas and drained the water off. I put the shrimp aside to cool, and sat at the table and watched while Marcy made a sauce.

Marcy looked up. "You're grinning like a cat."

"I wonder why."

"Maybe you like having a slave around."

"Is that why?" I asked.

"You want somebody to clean and cook…"

"I cooked the shrimp," I said.

"A warm body for your bed."

"I'm warm too."

Marcy grinned at me. "It's a silly conversation, isn't it?"

"Only if you believe that's all I want from you."

I was kissing her when the phone rang. I tried to say to hell with it, it couldn't be that important, but the phone kept ringing, and finally it was Marcy who stepped away from me.

It was Hump. "The Man just called. He says all hell just broke loose over at his place."

"Meet you there," I said. I got my .38 from the closet and my topcoat from the back of the sofa in the living room. Marcy stood in the kitchen doorway and watched while I struggled into the coat and dropped the .38 into the pocket. "Wait for me," I said. "I'll be back as soon as I can."

"What's wrong?"

"I don't know yet. I'll tell you when I get back."

I left before she could complain or ask me anything else.

Hump was there before me. He was at the rear of the building, with his back to the door that led to the staircase and up to The Man's apartment. When he recognized me he stepped away from the door. "It's a mess up there."

He opened the door and we went in. There was one body at the foot of the stairs. It was a black man who'd been with Ferd that night in front of the Dew Drop In. His hands were taped behind his back, and the back of his head had been blown away. I stepped around him and moved up the stairs to the top of the landing. There was another body there, and a pool of blood. This was a young white man, and he'd caught a load of shot in his chest and belly. His face hadn't been touched, except for some bluish spots where a few stray shot had hit him. He wasn't anybody I knew. A machine pistol poked out from under his body. I stepped over him and reached the closed door. The door had taken a burst or two from the machine pistol, and the lock and the wood around it were splintered. I tapped at the door.

"Hardman out here." The door eased open and I was looking into the eye of the pump gun. There was a different black behind it, one I didn't know. The pump gun waved past me and lined up on Hump, who was a step behind me. "Hump Evans is with me," I called out.

"Let them in." It was the flat voice of The Man.

Inside the living room, past the pump gun, the first thing I saw was the damage to the bar. A burst from the machine pistol had stitched across about four feet of the copper fronting. Another had slapped against a shelf of booze. The whole apartment smelled like good alcohol gone to waste.

The Man was sitting in a chair pulled away from the kitchen table. A white doctor, gray haired and distinguished and wearing a three-hundred-dollar suit, was bandaging The Man's right shoulder. The doctor didn't look too happy to see me. Maybe he thought I was a cop. He cleared his throat a couple of times like he wanted to speak, but he didn't say anything.

The Man looked at Hump and me. "It was a close one."

"I can read it from here," I said. "The black at the bottom of the stairs..."

"Horace," The Man said.

"...Horace went out for some reason..."

"Collecting," The Man said.

"...and he was picked up, and they tried to use him to get to you, to get past the door. But something went sour."

"Horace warned us."

"They'd come this far, so they tried to go on with it. The white with the machine pistol blew open the door and got off a burst or two before the pump gun got him."

"I keep forgetting you were a detective," The Man said.

"I'd say there was at least one other involved. One man doesn't try this kind of hit. It takes two or three."

"The other one hauled ass when the one on the landing got his." The Man nodded at the black with the pump gun. "J.T. thinks he's carrying lead too."

"What hit you?"

"Flying glass from the bar."

The doctor finished the taping and stepped away. He scribbled on a prescription pad. "I don't think you'll have much trouble with it, but it'll stiffen overnight." He put the prescription blank on the table and dropped the pad into the bag and closed it. "Get this filled. It's for the pain."

The Man got up and draped the smoking jacket over his shoulders like a cape. The doctor followed him out of the kitchen and into the living room. The doctor waited beside the bar while The Man went into the bedroom. The doctor caught me looking at him and looked away. The Man returned, and the doctor took the wad of bills uneasily, not liking to do it in front of me.

"Call my office tomorrow," the doctor said, going out and down the stairs. That's how doctors got rich, the unreported income. But I had a feeling this particular doctor might be busy the next time The Man called. There was too much blood and guts out there on the staircase.

"No police?" I asked.

The Man shook his head. "You two are my police."

"You know the one with the machine pistol?"

"No," The Man said. "I'd guess he was from out of town."

There were noises on the staircase, and J.T., the black with the pump gun, cracked the door and then swung it wide open. I stepped around him and saw two blacks in coveralls loading Horace into a movers' wardrobe box. Beyond them, I could see a van truck flush against the outside door. I went out to the landing and turned the dead white man over on his back. I pushed the machine pistol aside, and got my hands bloody doing it. I wiped my hands on the dead man's topcoat and spread it open. There was a .45 automatic in the waistband of his trousers. I pulled out the .45 and passed it back to Hump. Then I went over the dead man's clothes. In one pocket I found a money clip of bills and some change. I passed the bills and the change back to Hump. Hump handed them to The Man. I'd finished my look when the two blacks in coveralls came up the stairs with another wardrobe box. I straightened up and stepped away.

The Man stood watching the two blacks work, the bills fanned out in his hands. "Around four hundred dollars." He folded the money again and put the clip on. "Ape." One of the blacks looked up. "Split this up." He tossed the clip of money.

J.T. closed the door on their thanks. The Man moved to the bar and got three glasses. He poured out three heavy shots of scotch. He was waiting.

"Pros," I said. "No shop labels in the suit or the topcoat. From the weight of the topcoat, I'd say they were from out of town, maybe from the Midwest, where the winters are colder. Chicago or Detroit."

The Man nodded.

"The machine pistol's German, World War Two, probably brought back as a souvenir. Almost no way to trace it." I put out my hand and Hump put the .45 in it. "I'd make book that this is clean, too. The police might be able to trace it for a ways, but it would be a dead-end." I dropped the .45 on the bar counter and took the shot of scotch. "Who wants you dead this bad?"

"I don't know."

"You know," I said.

"I wish I did."

"Who was Emily afraid of? Who wants you dead, enough to pay the long-distance rates?"

"I don't know."

"That won't wash." Hump looked over the rim of his drink at The Man. "Late Monday night, a beginner tries Hardman. Two days later, the pros come after you. If the same man paid for both tries, then he must have learned you can't bank on beginners. He'd make a call early Tuesday morning, and the pros would be on the plane that afternoon. From Tuesday afternoon or evening to now, that's not much time to set things up."

I jumped into it. "That could mean two things. Whoever it is is in a hurry. They want you dead yesterday. Not next week. Otherwise, why storm the fort? The percentage isn't good. The percentage calls for a rifle on a rooftop, all neat and clean and safe, when you come out of the backdoor, or while you're walking across the parking lot to the car. Number two. Somebody knows your setup here. Somebody laid it all out for the two pros. Must have known when the collections were made. The whole hit hinged on picking up your bagman and using him to get inside."

The Man's face didn't show a thing.

"My guess is that it was somebody who hadn't been here the last few days. Probably didn't know about J.T. and the pump gun. That was the missing detail that screwed it up."

"They got the day's take," The Man said.

"How much?"

The Man shook his head. "Too much." The Man went into the kitchen and began dialing numbers and talking in a low voice. After a few minutes, he turned. "Horace got about halfway through the route."

"That backs it up. Somebody knew the whole route and picked the best spot, one where Horace could be taken without much risk."

"Hardman, it looks like somebody is after my operation."

I laughed at him. "Shit!" I said, "you're a funny man." And then I laughed some more. He didn't like it. To get rid of us, he said his shoulder was beginning to bother him. "I think I'd better go to bed." I said I'd stop by the next day. Maybe he'd have some sense by then. He didn't like that remark, either.

Out in the parking lot, we passed a panel truck with *Acme Cleaning and Repairs* on the side of it. Three blacks were taking a door from a frame on the side of the truck. That would replace the splintered one upstairs. I was sure they'd also scrub down the stairs when that was done. Unless I missed my guess, as soon as the stairs dried, they'd get a coat of paint.

A couple of blocks from The Man's apartment, I stopped at a closed service station that had an outside pay phone. Hump's car eased up behind me. I got Art at his department number.

"You pick up somebody with lead in them ... probably a shotgun wound?"

"Why?" When I didn't answer right away he said, "Involved with you?"

"I think so."

"You shoot somebody tonight?"

"No."

Art snorted. "I'm getting tired of this one-way street we've been running on. I'm not sure I can do it much longer."

"Come on, Art, I've told you all I could."

"I doubt that." There was a long pause. "Had a call about half an hour ago. Patrol car picked up a white male, around thirty, limping out along Whitehall. Good part of his side and hip were blown away. He says somebody shot him from a passing car. Said he didn't know who it was. Then he passed out."

"Where is he?"

"Grady emergency, last I heard."

"You looking into it?" I asked.

"I wasn't planning to, but …"

I said I'd meet him in the parking lot next to the emergency wing.

Hump got out of his car, stretching. He leaned on the door and watched as I walked over to him. "Any news?"

"They found the other gun, I think."

"Sooner or later," Hump said, "you're going to have to tell Art about The Man." I shook my head. "The later it is, the madder he's going to be."

"I can't do it yet. When this breaks wide open, he might not care." I told Hump I was going over to Grady. He could head on home and I'd call him later, after I'd seen the other gun.

Art was waiting for me in the strong glare of light at the emergency entrance platform. He looked like he'd been working himself up into a rage. I took my time walking up to him, stopping once to light a cigarette. That didn't help.

"All right, Hardman, tell me what it's about."

CHAPTER FIFTEEN

I saw that Art wasn't going to move until he got some kind of story out of me. I shivered and turned up my topcoat collar and began the tale I'd put together on the drive over to Grady.

"Had a tip …" I began.

"Where'd the tip come from?"

"Let me tell it all the way through. The tip said there were two pro guns from out of town. Chicago or Detroit … some place like that. They'd come to finish what Mullidge didn't. They were going to take me out tomorrow morning, when I stepped outside for the paper. But there was bad feeling between the two … over a girl, I think … and they got drunk and had a shoot. One got killed, and the other one was hit bad." I tossed the cigarette out into the parking lot. "That's all I heard."

"And you want …?"

"I want to know who's bringing the tourists in."

"God, you're a terrible liar," Art said.

Art showed his I.D., and one of the nurses on duty pointed him toward a screened area in the far right corner of the emergency room. A uniformed policeman was standing with his back to the screen, staring at the big rear-end of one of the nurses. When he saw Art approaching, he straightened up and became very official.

"How is he?" Art asked.

"Touch and go, the doc says."

Art stepped around the screen and I followed like a shadow. It was crowded back there. Two doctors and a nurse leaned over and the man on the table. Past an opening between their heads and shoulders, I could see the chewed-up, pulpy left side and hip. There was the strong smell of blood and guts, even over the stench of the disinfectant. I moved a couple of steps to the right, so that I could look down at the man's face. It was a dark, pockmarked face with blue-black five o'clock shadow. His eyes were closed, the lips barely quivering.

One of the doctors stepped away from the table and dropped a probe in a pan. He turned toward Art and Art flipped his I.D. "How is he?"

The doctor shook his head. "Hard to say. He almost bled to death before they got him here. I've done all I can here. We've called in an operating team."

"The chances?"

"Fifty-fifty."

"Can we talk to him a minute or two?" Art asked.

"If he'll talk to you," the doctor said. "He wouldn't even tell us his name."

The doctor nodded at the other doctor, and they went around us and out through the screen. The nurse remained behind, moving here and there, straightening up.

Art leaned over the man on the table. "Gunner."

That surprised me, and then I realized that that was as good a name as any to get his attention.

"Hardman's here, the one you were supposed to kill."

The man's eyes blinked open. He had trouble keeping them open, as if he couldn't focus them.

"Gunner..."

"Call me John Doe." The lips curled.

"This is Hardman, the one you were after," Art said.

"Who's...he?"

"You not after him?"

I stepped closer to the table. "Who paid you?"

The eyes shifted from Art over to me. "Just...passing...through town."

"Who paid you?" Art said.

"Fuck you." The man closed his eyes and turned his face away from us. Art asked some more questions, but it was just wind down the tunnel. As far as the man was concerned, we weren't there. Or he'd passed out. Either way, we didn't get any more answers from him. Art gave up. It would have to wait until he was either better or very much worse.

From the desk, Art called the department and asked them to send over a fingerprint man. "He's probably got a record as long as a leg." Before I left, we went over his things. It was just like it was with the dead man on The Man's landing. A wad of bills, some change, a pack of cigarettes and a wickedly sharp switchblade.

Art followed me out to the parking lot. "That tip say where this shoot took place?"

"No," I said.

"Call back and ask. There's a body missing."

"I don't know where the tip came from."

"I didn't think you would," Art said. "It takes all the fun out of guessing, when you tell me something."

"Sorry."

"If I don't get some answers soon, your old friend, the cop, is gonna leave town. The next time I talk to you, I'll be the cop who used to be your friend."

I nodded.

The nod made him mad. "Don't just nod at me. This town looks like a fucking Asian war's going on in it. And you're not helping."

There wasn't anything I could say.

When I drove away, he was still standing in the parking lot, head back and, I thought, cursing. It was a mess and, as he'd said,

I wasn't doing much to improve it. It wasn't hard to understand how he felt.

The radio was giving the eleven o'clock news when I drove up the driveway and parked. From outside the door, I could hear the TV. news going, and I found Marcy curled up on the sofa. She uncoiled and stood up in her stocking feet, waiting for me. "See how patient I am."

I swept her up and kissed her and walked her into the kitchen. "It's been a bad evening," I said when I released her, "so I'm glad you are."

I opened the Inglenook Chablis, and she got out the shrimp and the sauce, and we ate while I told her what had happened. At a break, while Marcy made coffee, I went into the bedroom and made two calls. Hump said he wasn't surprised that the gunner wouldn't talk. That was part of the contract. And, with his story about being shot from a passing car, he wasn't guilty of anything but being in the wrong place at the wrong time.

The Man sounded relieved. "I guess I can relax for the moment," he said. "If they're going to try again, it'll take time to set it up."

I agreed. "But the body count being what it is, if they do make another try, it'll be the safe way, a high-powered rifle at a distance."

"Hardman, you don't go out of your way to reassure me, do you?"

"If you want to be dead," I said, "I'll lie to you."

He laughed, but it wasn't a real laugh. "I'll have to think on this overnight."

I got out the bottle of five-star Metaxa to go with the coffee. Marcy seemed subdued. Perhaps it was the way I'd told my story and then left her to think about it while I made my phone calls. "I guess this is what they call a late supper in all the movies," I said.

She sipped at the Metaxa and looked at me like I'd said nothing at all. "So that's the kind of work you do now, Jim?"

"Yes, and it's pretty dirty at times."

"It doesn't sound exactly honest," Marcy said.

"Sometimes it's not." I topped off my Metaxa. "But it's not like pimping, or working full-time for a mob."

"The Man ... whoever he is ... he sounds like the Black Mafia. You're working for him."

"It's not the same thing," I said. "I'm not a bagman for him. I'm investigating a murder. It's The Man's personal life I'm involved in, not his business life."

"You believe that, Jim?"

I grinned at her and shook my head. "It started that way. Now I'm not sure. Maybe there are two parts here that aren't connected. The murder of Emily Campbell might have nothing to do with the other killings around The Man. But I think they do. I just don't know the connection."

"And when you know the connection?" Marcy asked.

"Then I throw it all to Art, and stand back and watch."

"Or help him."

"Or, if he wants me to, I help him," I said.

Marcy rinsed her cup and left it in the sink. One hip against the kitchen counter, she sipped at the Metaxa. "You didn't drink this before, when you were going with me?"

"An old Greek man I met in a bar said it was good for your virility. At least, I think that was what he said."

"Really?" She smiled at me, licking her lips. "You?"

"It was just a theory. I never tried it out."

Marcy stayed the night and left early the next morning by cab, while I was still asleep. I found a note on the dresser, weighted down by some change. *Only two shopping days until Christmas. Marcy*

I was on my third cup of coffee when a man from one of the messenger services came by. For my signature, he gave me a thick, sealed envelope with my name and address on it. Though it was something like paying too much for a grab-bag prize, I had him wait while I got a dollar for him from the bedroom.

At the kitchen table I opened the envelope, and a sheaf of cash and a note fell out. I put the cash aside and read the letter.

"After the trouble last night I've decided to take a vacation. I'll be out of the country for a time. Now and then an associate, a Mr. Wenzel Brown, will contact you for a progress report. I do not plan to return until the trouble has cleared up, or until I am sure it has died down. Though I trust you to some degree, I feel my whereabouts should be kept secret from everyone not in my organization. The enclosed money should retain your services for another period of time. Other cash, as needed, will be available from Mr. Brown, and we will settle up any differences when I return to town."

There wasn't a signature. I didn't need one. I counted the cash and found there was a thousand dollars in twenties and fifties. I put it into two equal stacks and went into the bedroom. I put in a call to The Man's number, but there was no answer. I figured that. He'd left the night before or very early in the morning.

That tore it. Here I was, working for a client who'd blown town, leaving me with a lot of dead people I couldn't explain, and Art Maloney who wanted an explanation more than he wanted my friendship. Not that I blamed The Man, goddamit. Under the same gun, I guess I'd have done the same thing. And after I got over the feeling that I was on shaky ground and that he'd put me there, I'd probably end up hoping The Man had covered his tracks well enough so another crew of gunners couldn't find him.

I dialed Hump's number. "We've got another payday over here. Why don't you drop by, and we'll try to find some way to earn it."

Hump said he'd be by within the hour.

I showered and shaved, and was dressed and tying my shoelaces when Art called. "You got anything to tell me, Hardman?"

"Maybe by Christmas," I said.

"You might be in jail by then."

"Lord, I hope not," I said, "Marcy might not understand that."

"That's a low hit. I'm going to tell Edna on you." But he sounded a bit looser, like he'd gotten over part of the night before. "Two things. Gunner died in intensive care last night, after the operation."

"Another dead-end alley," I said.

"Number two. I finally got around to doing some more of your work. You wanted to know why Mullidge didn't get his day in court."

"I thought you'd forgotten about that."

"It took time. I had to find a man."

I cradled the phone between my neck and shoulder and tied both shoelaces. "And ...?"

"It was fixed by a big-time lawyer named Ernest Lockridge. Has an office downtown. I didn't get the address, but I figured you might have a phone book."

I said I did.

"Work fast, Hardman, my patience's about gone." He hung up.

Hump folded his share of The Man's money and put a rubber band on it. "This thing lasts much longer, I might retire."

"Not the way you live." I got out a couple of bottles of Beck's, and we drank them standing up in the kitchen. "This Ernest Lockridge, you know anything about him?"

"Seen his picture in the paper now and then. Always winning some local golf tournament, or heading up some fund drive or other."

"Why would he be putting out clout for some nickel-dime day worker?" I asked.

"He wouldn't," Hump said, "unless he was doing it for somebody else."

"Which means there's about a one-in-five chance that he might know somebody who doesn't like me."

"Might be two-in-five or three-in-five," Hump said. "And, if he's nasty enough, he might even have fingered you with Mullidge."

"I've got to meet this fellow."

"Wouldn't miss it," Hump said, throwing back his head and pouring down the last of the Beck's.

I parked at Rich's, and we rode the elevator down to the street level. We walked over the two blocks to the Peachtree Business Tower. The directory in the lobby gave Lockridge's office as 1212. It was a fancy lobby, though it was one of the older downtown buildings. It was done in gray marble and black tile, and had a kind of old-style wrought-iron trim. It wasn't until we stepped off the elevator on the 12th floor that I realized the lobby was just a front, that it had been recently renovated, while the rest of the building was probably a slum. The hallway carpeting had bare spots, some of the paint on the walls was flaking, and the bulbs in some of the overhead fixtures needed changing. It didn't seem like a place where big clout lived, after all.

We found 1212 and went in. An aging secretary looked up at us with her teeth sunk into a ham and cheese on rye, and blinked her eyes in shock. She looked like she'd been, ten or fifteen years ago, the kind of secretary who didn't need to know how to type or take shorthand. Now, though she was holding it together with paste and rubber bands, I had the feeling that she'd been over to the night schools recently.

I said I wanted to see Ernest Lockridge.

She took the sandwich out of her mouth, the bite marks still there, and said, "He's not in right now. The legislature's in session."

I looked at Hump. His nod meant that we were thinking the same thing. All the arrows seemed to be pointing toward the Capitol and the offices over there.

"When do you expect him?"

"He usually comes in by three or three-thirty."

"We'll come back then."

"Would you like to leave your name, and tell me the nature of your business with Mr. Lockridge?"

"Not really," I said. "It's too awful to tell to a lady."

We left her looking down at the sandwich, as if trying to decide whether she wanted to bite into the same tooth marks again. Hump and I spent the early part of the afternoon over lunch. It was bitter outside, so we decided not to walk down to Peachtree Center and watch the girls go by. It just wasn't the same in the winter, when they were all wearing heavy coats.

At three-fifteen, we presented ourselves at the office once more. She must have heard us coming, because she was typing away when we entered. She finished a paragraph before she looked up at us.

I gave her a phony name. Ben Blackmond.

"Mr. Lockridge is in now, but he's very busy. Unless you have an appointment, or unless you're willing to tell me the nature of your ..."

"You can tell him," I said, "that it's an investigation about a bribery case."

"Then you're policemen?"

I didn't say I was or wasn't. I didn't even nod. I just looked at her with the hardest stare I had.

"You should have told me when you were here before." She fluttered around her desk and into the inner office. A minute later she came out again and held the door open for us.

Ernest Lockridge was one of those so-handsome young men who was now going to seed. He'd reached forty and gone past it, and the forties had hit him a good lick that had stunned him. The workouts at the health club and the minutes under the sunlamp couldn't do anything about the wrinkles and the second chin that was beginning to droop a little over his Brooks Brothers shirt and tie.

"You said it was about a bribery case you're investigating."

"I said it was about a bribery case," I said.

"But you're not investigating it?" Lockridge had a pencil in his hand, tapping the point against the desk blotter and then reversing it and tapping the eraser.

"You handled a theft-from-auto case for a Fred Mullidge, a bit over a year ago."

"I have handled a lot of cases in the past year." But the pencil stopped in the middle of the reverse, between point and eraser.

"The case wasn't tried."

"That happens fairly often," Lockridge said, the pencil moving again. "The charges get dropped when the police find out they don't have the case they thought they had."

"Who hired you to defend Mullidge?"

"I assume Mullidge did."

"You're not sure?" I asked.

"It was Mullidge."

"That's better." I turned to Hump. "Don't you think that's better?"

"A straight answer's better than a crooked one," Hump said.

"How do we know it's a straight answer?"

Lockridge dropped the pencil into a holder and tightened his jaw. "I think you'd better show me some identification now."

I looked at him and smiled.

"Then you aren't policemen?"

"That was your guess."

"Miss Barker said ..."

"That was her guess, too," I said.

"You'll have to leave then. I have no more time for questions and answers. It's not a game I especially like."

I nodded. "That's your right, of course. But I think you can expect another visitor in the next day or two."

"Another visitor ...?"

"A real cop," I said.

As soon as we stepped through the doorway into the outer office, Lockridge slammed the door behind us. Hump got his coat and scarf from the rack and put them on. He was ready to go, and he looked a bit puzzled at how slow I was. I leaned toward him and said, under my breath, "Keep her quiet." I indicated the secretary and Hump nodded. The secretary was typing away like mad, not watching us at all. I fished out a cigarette and held it up as I approached her desk. Hump started out beside me, but when I was flush against the desk, he drifted to the side and circled the desk.

"Got a match? I seem to be out."

"I think so." She reached for one of the desk drawers and, at that moment, Hump slipped a big hand over her mouth. The other hand clamped her shoulder, pushing her down and holding her in the chair.

"Nobody's going to hurt you," I said. I reached across the desk and lifted the phone from its cradle.

"... afraid he's not in his office now. The legislature's adjourned for Christmas. I'm not sure he'll be back in until after January First. Would you like to leave a message, in case he does…?"

Lockridge cut in. "No, it's nothing important. Thank you."

They hung up, and I replaced the phone. I looked at the secretary's wide, frightened eyes. "Now he's going to take his hand away. Don't scream. You won't scream, will you?"

She shook her head.

When Hump pulled his hand away and stepped back, she dropped her head on the desk and shuddered. Hump and I went out of the office at a fast walk. We passed up the elevator and walked up two flights. There we stood around the elevator as if we were waiting for it. Ten minutes passed that way, and then we caught an elevator and rode it down to the basement parking area. It was a single-level parking deck that didn't hold more than fifty cars. I'd intended to go out that way, but when I saw the attendant heading for us I got another idea.

"What you want down here?" the attendant said.

I got out my wallet and found another one of those Nationwide Insurance cards I'd been giving away so freely in the last week or so. I handed it to him and, while he read it, asked, "Ernest Lockridge keep his car down here?"

"Sure, Mr. Lockridge does."

"Which one's his?"

"The '71 Skylark, the blue one over there." He tagged along with us. "What's wrong."

"Tell you about it in a minute." When we reached the Skylark, I got out my pad and wrote down the license number. Then I walked around front and checked the right front fender. "Not a mark on it," I said to Hump. "How do you like that?"

"I didn't think we'd find one," Hump said, but he was looking at me like he didn't know what the plot was, and he'd appreciate a clue.

"Barker lied to us," I said.

"I trusted him," Hump said. "That just goes to show you."

I closed my pad and put it away. The attendant was still waiting around for his explanation. I went over to him. Hump followed and towered over both of us.

"A client of mine got a fender scraped the other night in *a* parking lot outside of the San Souci. He said the other driver didn't stop, but he got this license number."

"He probably hit a wall," Hump said.

"That's right," I said, "and he just made up this number to try to get himself off the hook."

"Drinking again, I bet," Hump said.

"Now he'll say he must have missed a number, or got one wrong." I shook my head sadly and palmed a five-dollar bill. Hump turned away as I dropped it into the attendant's hand. "Don't say anything about this to Mr. Lockridge. Barker's in enough trouble for lying to us."

"Sure," the attendant said. "My mind's a blank."

I made a note of where the parking lot exited, and Hump and I went up to the lobby and walked back to Rich's, to get my Ford. I drove back to the Peachtree Business Tower and circled the block until I found the ramp from the lot. There wasn't a parking space, but I found a Loading-Unloading area and waited there.

"If he hasn't already left," Hump said. "He might have."

"First he's got to calm his secretary down."

"That ought to take twenty minutes and two tranquilizers."

"An important fellow like him," I said, "he might even have another appointment."

"I've got one question."

"Yes, Hump?"

"Why are we following him around, anyway?"

"You got something better to do?"

Hump shook his head. "Not tonight."

"Lockridge didn't reach his man, and I think we might have made him nervous enough to lead us somewhere we want to go."

"You think so?"

"Who knows? Anyway, I'd do anything to keep from going Christmas shopping."

It was cold, and the wind was whipping down the channels formed by the high office buildings. The shoppers passing by looked like they were angry with themselves for coming out in the first place. The parcels were big and fat, and you knew the pocketbooks were thin and empty. Four-thirty came and went, and still there was no sign of Lockridge. Around five, Hump spotted a liquor store a few doors down and decided that we could use something in the way of a body warmer. I gave him a five and asked him to pick up a half pint of Hennessey cognac for me. And to watch the street in case I pulled up in pursuit of Lockridge.

It almost worked that way. At five, the cars began to come down the ramp and into the street. So far, no sign of the blue Skylark. It was a slow stream, minutes apart, and then, just as Hump came out of the liquor store, the blue Skylark dipped out of the ramp and turned on the one-way street. Hump saw the Skylark the same time I did, and moved quickly to put his back to the street. I kept my head up just long enough to be sure that Lockridge was driving, and then I ducked and put my head against the seat. I did a slow count to ten and, when I looked up, Lockridge was ahead of me, moving into the right-turn lane. I kicked the engine over and waited until Hump was in the car. Then I followed. Hump unscrewed the cap from the Hennessey and passed it to me, while I kept my eyes on the Skylark. I had a swallow and felt it burn all the way down to my toes, and then the steam came out of my ears. It was welcome, burn and steam, after sitting in the cold car.

It was a roundabout route. I couldn't seem to get the real destination fixed in my mind. I think it was the traffic rather then any evasive plan on the part of Lockridge. Perhaps it was a way he'd worked out that would get him where he was going in less time, with less hassle, but it kept me jumping. I stayed back a car and sometimes two cars. In time, it turned out that he'd gone around about a hundred and eighty degrees, and was now headed into Northeast Atlanta.

As we passed through the tight-squeeze area, I put out my hand and Hump put the half-pint flask of cognac in it. I had another sip and passed it back. Hump capped it and stacked it away in the glove box. At Fifteenth, just before we reached the High Museum, Lockridge took a right and we followed through a maze of dark, curving streets until, making one tight curve, I saw the Skylark ahead on the left. Lockridge was making a U-turn and I thought, oh, shit, now what's he doing? But before we reached the Skylark, it had stopped and Lockridge was getting out.

"See where he goes," I said. Just as we drew even with Lockridge, I turned my head away from him, as if looking for something across the street.

"He's going up the walk to that white stucco back there. He's inside."

At that, I found a driveway and pulled in. I backed around and eased my Ford into the curb two houses before the white stucco. The house had two floors. There were no lights burning on the bottom floor and, as we watched, another light went on, adding to the ones already lit on the second floor.

I shivered and looked over at Hump. "What do you think it is, apartments?"

"Hard to tell."

"And hard to find out." I got out and buttoned up my topcoat. In case anyone was watching, I did a charade that was supposed to convince them I was looking at house numbers. I felt a little foolish doing it, especially on such a cold night, but I didn't want to run the risk that somebody might notice our car and think we were prowlers. I didn't want anybody to call the police just yet. If at all.

I reached the white stucco house and went up the narrow walkway that led to the entrance. In the entranceway it was half darkness, lit only by the lights from the short hallway beyond. On the left wall there were two mailboxes and buzzer systems. I got out my lighter and read the name cards over the buzzers by its flicker. The first card was engraved: *Mr. and Mrs. Henry Armitage* and, typed below that, *Apt. No. 1, Ground Floor.* The other card, printed with a felt-tip pen, gave the occupant as *Alice Jarman* and beneath that, *Apt. No. 2, 2nd Floor.*

I returned to the car. Hump passed me the glass flask of Hennessey and waited while I had a swallow. "Hump, do you know if Lockridge is married?"

"Not sure."

"I think he's up there with some girl named Alice Jarman. If she's his fuck away from home, we might have a lever on him."

"She might be his Aunt Alice," Hump said.

"Or his hot crotch."

"So what's next?" Hump asked.

"There's a 7-11 store two blocks back. Ought to be a pay phone there. Call the Lockridge number, the home listing. Put on your best Uncle Tom, and tell Mrs. Lockridge you do yard work and clean gutters and downspouts."

"In other words, find out if there is a Mrs. Lockridge?"

"Right."

"Walking?" Hump asked.

"Sorry," I said, "but I want to follow him if he comes out while you're gone."

Hump opened the car door. "And if you're gone when I get back?"

"Having tried out your Uncle Tom on Mrs. Lockridge, you could fake it again with Alice."

"You want to know if she's eighty or twenty."

I nodded. "And bring back something to eat."

He closed the door. I watched him stride down the street, looking like every Southern white lady's black-rape nightmare. The way he walked, it wouldn't take him long. I figured about ten minutes, each way. Maybe a couple of minutes for the phone call. So twenty-five minutes. If Alice was the hot crotch, I could figure on Lockridge being there for a time. At least that long. Hell, he looked corrupt enough to like it with whips.

Ten minutes passed. I got out the Hennessey and sipped at it. Now and then a car would pass, but I'd see the lights in time and flatten out across the seat.

I'd cracked the window on the passenger side. Otherwise I might not have heard it. It was a distant *pop, pop, pop,* like somebody breaking balloons. I slid to the passenger side and looked up. Perhaps I'd have written it off, but with the next pop there was the tinkle of glass, and the front right window on the second floor broke, and I could see the shattered pane with the lights behind it.

I was out of the car on a run. I cut across lawns and jumped one low hedge. I reached the white stucco house and did the steps two at a time. The door to the hallway was locked. I tried to force it with my shoulder and, when that didn't work, I got my gun out and broke the window section of the door with the butt and reached in. I got the inside doorknob and twisted it, and I was in the hallway, skidding on the glass fragments, and then getting my balance and springing for the stairs. I knew I was making too much noise, and my breathing hurt. After the run, my legs weren't steady. Goddamn middle age, anyway! But I kept going, using the banister, until I reached the landing. Ahead of me was a narrow walkway or hall, with the banister to my right and the stairwell below it; on my left was a wall unbroken by doors. The main door was at the end of the walkway, and I was halfway there when the lights went out. It must have been one of those two-way switches, activated from inside the apartment.

The door opened, but there was no light in the apartment beyond. I braced myself and started to bring my gun up. At that moment, the man ran into me. I caught the smell of shaving lotion and tobacco and sweat, and the soft brush of tweed across my face. A knee or a fist hit me about waist high, and the wind went out of me. I tried to bring the gun up, but something hit my right shoulder, and my whole arm went numb. The gun flew out of my hand, and I heard it land on the stairwell below. I swung at him with my left hand and missed, but my hand grabbed cloth and held on. At the same time, I felt a hand on the back of my neck pushing my head down. The cloth I held onto tore, and something struck me on the back of the head. The tearing seemed to go on, and I thought it was my skin tearing that I heard. I felt myself falling, and there must have been a second blow on my head. Maybe there was even a third. The last thing I felt was the rough carpet slapping against the side of my face.

CHAPTER SIXTEEN

I was still in the hallway, but pushed to one side. I felt the wall all down my right side. People were passing me, going both ways, and a dark shape loomed over me, blotting out the light. There was wet cloth on my face, and the top of my head was throbbing to my heartbeat.

"Hardman, Hardman, you all right?"

"Hump?"

"Yeah."

"I feel like God's worst hangover." I tried to push myself up into a sitting position. "Help me up."

Hump pulled me to my feet and steadied me. I was dizzy, and the throbbing in my head got worse, and I thought I was going to throw up. I choked it down, feeling the bubble of vomit just below the back of my throat. But it stayed down. "Art here?"

"Inside." Hump led me into the apartment. The lights were too bright there, and I stood blinking until Art came over.

"Back with us, huh?" Art took my other arm and they led me over to a soft chair and sat me down. While Art made notes, I told them what had happened after Hump had left to go the 7-11 store. When I was done, I said, "Picked up Lockridge yet?"

"As soon as the meat wagon gets here," Art said.

I'd been looking at the form on the floor. It was covered with a sheet, but a woman's feet and shoes stuck out at the bottom. "I thought…"

"Alice Jarman or whoever she is got it in here. Lockridge got as far as the front bedroom. One of the shots that got him must have broken the windowpane, and the one you heard. The way we read it, the girl got it first, once in the chest and once in the head. Lockridge made a run for the bedroom, got hit once on the way, and then got hit three more times, including one in the back of the head."

"Six shots," Hump said, "and maybe no time to reload."

"That might be why you're still alive," Art said. He reached into his topcoat pocket and brought out a wad of cloth. "Hump found this in your hand."

"I remember a tearing sound, but I thought that was my head." I got the wad of cloth and spread it out. It was the inside pocket from a jacket or a coat. *J. Mabry. Atlanta, Charlotte, Richmond.* I passed it to Art and he dropped it into his pocket once more. "Very exclusive place. Do a background check on you before they even consider tailoring for you. Don't want their clothes to be worn by gangsters or disreputable people."

"I've called the manager. He's staying after closing hours." Art looked at his watch. "He's expecting me now. You got anybody you want checked our? Anybody you think might have their tailoring done by Mabry?"

"Two," I said. "No, make that three. Ben Coleman, Hugh Muffin and Arch Campbell."

"Muffin, your client?"

"Just because he's my client doesn't mean he walks on water." I shook my head. "Whoever it was must be built like a fullback. Muffin's too old and soft, and so is Campbell."

"That leaves Coleman," Hump said.

Art closed his notebook with a loud smack. "First, let's see what Mabry has. Where you going to be, Hardman?"

"Emergency room, first," Hump said. "Then his place."

"While you're there," I said after Art, "see about one of their three hundred and fifty dollar bargain suits."

At the doorway, Art turned and gave me the finger.

After the hospital, where a patch of hair was shaved and a few stitches taken on my scalp, Hump drove me home. I told Hump to look in the cabinet for the J&B, and I went into the bedroom and called Marcy. She wanted to come over but I told her, in the shape I was in, I'd be the worst gentleman suitor around, and how about Christmas Eve instead? She said fine, and I said I'd call her.

Hump sat at the kitchen table with the bottle of J&B and a glass. My flask of Hennessey was on the table, next to my .38.

"Found it on the stairs," Hump said.

I got myself a shot glass and drank a bit of the cognac. "Anybody around when you got there?"

"Nobody in the neighborhood even cracked a window. Talk about New York City, and that woman getting killed in the courtyard. Shit! There could have been a war in the street, and nobody'd have looked."

"I can't blame them." I touched the taped patch on the back of my head. "Look what it got me."

"It could have got you dead." Hump went to the refrigerator and looked in. "We never did have any supper. Your head might be dulling your appetite, but mine's still sharp."

"Pack of roast beef in the foil."

"Got it." Hump loaded up the table with the sandwich and snack stuff I'd bought to replace the spoiled food from Eddie Spence's visit about five or six days before. "About your head. I thought you lost it back there."

"Maybe." I reached across and picked off a slice of roast beef.

"Maybe, shit! Charging upstairs into a gun fight … by yourself."

I chewed on the beef. "I guess it was impulsive of me." It was hard forcing it down, but I wanted something in my stomach. "If I had it to do over, I might sit down in the dark yard and wait for him to come to me. Unless he went out the back door, and left me with egg on my face."

"Better than a bullet in it."

Art called. "Hardman, you got two out of three, and an *almost* on the third. Hugh Muffin's been a customer for about ten years, Ben Coleman for about two years, and Arch Cambell just made application."

"Where are you?"

"At the department, trying to get a search warrant for Coleman's apartment. If it's Coleman, I want to get there before he has a chance to get rid of the coat."

"Where's his apartment?"

"The Mesa Verde apartments, 8 E." A pause. "Why?"

"I can't sleep. Hump and I'll drive over there and sit out front until you get there."

"Sure you're up to it?"

"What's ten stitches, more or less?"

"All right," Art said, "but don't flush him."

"I've got this idea," I said. "I'm the one with the busted head, right?"

"Right."

"Before you get there, Hump and I could talk to him. With me, he can't ask for his lawyer."

"Or choose to remain silent," Art said.

"People just look at Hump and start talking."

"See you there."

The door to 8E opened a few inches. Ben Coleman squinted out at us, then flicked on the porch lights. "What do you want, Hardman?"

"I wanted to talk to you about the reward."

"Not tonight," Coleman said. "Come and see me in the morning and …"

Hump stepped around me and put his shoulder to the door. Coleman fell away from the door and we went inside. Hump closed the door and put on the chain lock. Coleman, in a bathrobe and pajamas, watched this with a hard eye. "I'm not sure the police will …"

"That's tomorrow," I said. "Right now, the police don't have anything to do with it." I gave Hump a nod. "You know what we're looking for."

Hump moved around Coleman and went into the bedroom. Coleman turned his head, following Hump, and then looked back at me. "You know this is an illegal search."

"As illegal as it can get," I said. "But I'm not the police, so it won't get to court."

"What's that supposed to mean?" He sounded angry, but there was a lot of bluff in it.

"What it sounds like." I looked around the room. "You got a drink?"

"Over there." He pointed to a cabinet near the bedroom door. "I think there's a vague threat in this somewhere."

"It's not vague." I got out a glass and a bottle of Walker Red. "Let's just say I'm pissed, and I've got a lump on my head and a headache. That's enough for me."

"Enough for what?"

"So I won't lose sleep if you end up in a garbage dump somewhere."

"That's not funny." Under his winter tan, he'd paled some.

"Who's trying to be funny?"

The rattling around in the bedroom ended with the slamming of a door, and Hump came back in. "Lots of suits and sport coats with the Mabry label. None with a torn pocket."

I sipped at the scotch and looked at Coleman. "Find a tweed topcoat?"

"No topcoat in there, tweed or otherwise."

Coleman dropped his eyes.

"That's strange, isn't it? A well-dressed fellow like this without a topcoat." I motioned at the bottle of Walker Red. "Be his guest, Hump."

"Why not?" He poured himself a big shot. "He's not going to need it."

Coleman jerked his eyes open. "I know you're bluffing. You just don't go around killing people in cold blood."

"Mine's not cold at the moment." I held out my glass and Hump topped it off. "No topcoat, huh?"

"It's at the cleaners."

"Which one?"

His lips moved, but nothing came out for a few seconds. "The one on Briarcliff. I forget the name."

"That's a fat lie," Hump said. "He tossed it out of the car somewhere."

I watched his eyes. Nothing.

"Or it's in the incinerator," I said.

His eyes. Still nothing. "Or in the trunk of his car." I watched his eyes and he blinked. That might not mean much, but it was worth a try. "See if you can find his car keys."

"They're on the dresser," Hump said. "I saw them a second ago."

While Hump was in the bedroom, I leaned over Coleman. "Which car's yours?"

"You know so much, you find it."

"Smartass." I hit him across the mouth with my open hand. "But I think you're telling me something, Ben."

His tongue licked at the left corner of his mouth. I must have cut the inside of his mouth. "That kind of search, it'll never stand up in court."

"I keep losing you. I don't think you're listening. You're the one who keeps talking about this going to court, not me." I slugged down the rest of my drink and got out my handkerchief. Without looking at him I wiped the glass and put it back in the cabinet. "I just want to be sure in my mind before I do anything rash."

"Here they are." Hump tossed me the car keys.

I looked down at the half-dozen or so keys and the miniature license tag. "It's better you don't help us, anyway. This way, I can keep my mad going." I read off the tag numbers to Hump and tossed the keys back to him. "It ought to be out front, probably on this side of the street."

I heard a couple of car doors slam out front. I went to the front window and looked out. Art was coming up the walk with two uniformed cops.

"No help," I said to Coleman. "It's a friend."

I unhooked the chain lock and let Art in. "Coleman hasn't been too helpful."

"His scotch is okay, though," Hump said.

"The search warrant you've got," I asked, "does that cover his car too?"

All nodded. He showed the warrant to Coleman. I tossed him the keys. "I think the topcoat's in his trunk."

"Which is your car?" Art asked.

Coleman shook his head.

"You see? Not helpful. The tag numbers are on the key chain."

"Oh, what the hell," Coleman said. "It's the tan Dodge."

"That's more like it." Art sent the two uniformed cops out to search the car trunk. He closed the outside door and leaned his back against it. "Why'd you kill Lockridge and the girl?"

"I didn't kill the girl or Lockridge."

"The coat with the torn-off pocket, that'll place you there. That's step one. We'll build up the rest of it." Art looked at me. "We could make a love triangle out of it. You and Lockridge had it out over the girl. You got mad and killed both of them."

"I hardly knew the girl," Coleman said.

"I've got a witness who'll say otherwise," Art said. "Right, Jim?"

"Sure." I grinned at Coleman. "I was following you. In my notebook, I've got four or five times you went over to the Jarman girl's place around midnight and stayed until the next morning."

"Anything else?" Art asked.

"You mean something that'll give us a motive? Let's see. How's this? One night, I heard Coleman and this Alice girl having a hell of an argument in a parking lot. Coleman was saying he knew she was seeing Lockridge, and she'd better stop it or else." I winked at Hump, letting Ben Coleman see me doing it. "You got any idea what parking lot that was, Hump?"

"It'd be a high-class place," Hump said. "The Chateau, maybe."

"That was it, the Chateau."

"That ties it up," Art said. "Relationship with the girl, motive for the killings and, with the topcoat, we place you there, Coleman. That's murder one."

"You're serious?" Coleman looked like he might faint. "You really serious?"

"That's my case." Art nodded toward me. "What do you think, Jim?"

"I'd buy it. And to strengthen it, we'll add Hump. Hump'll say he was with me two or three times."

"Right." Hump laughed. "I was with you that night outside the Chateau when he had the shout-out with the girl, and I was with you twice when you had the girl's apartment staked out. Coleman, you stayed to breakfast both times."

"Art, you'll get a citation for breaking this one," I said.

"It was easy," Art said. "The wonder is, it took as long as it did. I should have known two hours ago."

"It wasn't me," Coleman choked out. I could barely hear him.

"Speak up," Art said. "I can't hear you."

"I didn't do it. Hugh Muffin did."

Lockridge reached Hugh at a cocktail party at the Regency, around four-thirty. Lockridge was in such a panic that Hugh could hardly understand him. There was something about two men coming by asking questions about Mullidge, and saying that the police would be by to ask the same questions. And they'd frightened his secretary into a mild case of shock. To calm him, Hugh said he'd meet Lockridge right away, and they'd settled on Alice Jarman's apartment. It was a safe meeting place they'd used before. Hugh and Coleman arrived first and parked down the street. They had a drink with Alice Jarman, and Lockridge appeared not long after them. At first, it seemed that Hugh had it under control, that he had Lockridge snowed. It turned out that it wasn't that way at all. Lockridge was frayed around the edges. He kept saying that his only connection with the case was that he'd gotten Mullidge off on the theft-from-auto charge. He wasn't about to take any of the rap for murder. Yes, he knew about the murder of the girl, and he wasn't about to …

That was when Hugh went berserk. He pulled his hand from his pocket and there was a gun in it. The girl got in the way and took the first slug, and she went down hard. Hugh winged Lockridge as he ran for the bedroom, and then Hugh followed him into the bedroom and finished him off. He was still in the bedroom when Coleman got over the panic and shock. He was afraid that Hugh would kill him, too, and that was when he switched off the lights and made a run for it. It was then, out in the hallway, that he ran into Hardman. He got by Hardman, but not without losing part of his topcoat. The rest of it was out of the same nightmare. He'd come over in Hugh's car, and now he had run for what seemed like miles until he reached a service station. He got a cab and rode downtown to the Regency, where he picked up his car. On the drive home, he discovered the torn inside pocket of the topcoat. When he reached the apartment, he locked the topcoat away in the trunk of his car while he tried to decide what to do with it. Whether to destroy it or try to have it repaired.

And hardly an hour ago, Hugh Muffin had called. Coleman thought he'd convinced Hugh that he had no intention of going to the police. He'd just been shocked back there at the apartment: it was the first time he'd ever seen anybody killed.

"But that was a lie, wasn't it?" I said. "You were going to be a good citizen the whole time."

Coleman nodded. "Hugh's crazy when he's like that. You can't talk to him or reason with him."

"Emily Campbell," I said. "What about her?"

"I don't know. Hugh killed her or he had her killed. It might have been Mullidge."

Art said, "It wasn't Hugh himself. He was iron-clad, at a dinner party from eight to around one that night."

"Mullidge then." I turned back to Coleman. "What was the tie between Hugh and Mullidge and Lockridge?"

It was a long story. Hugh's office had been one of those that Mullidge had stolen from while he worked as a janitor for the state. The articles taken hadn't been especially valuable, but Hugh had nosed around and decided that it had to be the cleaning crew. He waited in his office and confronted Mullidge. Mullidge cracked wide open under pressure. He thought he was headed for jail. Instead, it turned out that Hugh wanted him to continue stealing from selected offices. It was always good to know what was going on in other parts of the building. For a time, it worked well. Mullidge would steal documents and letters and return them the next day, before they were missed. At the same time, against Hugh's warning, Mullidge continued to steal other things. When the pressure got bad, Hugh advised Mullidge to find another job. That led to the parking lot job. Hugh continued to use Mullidge from time to time, when he needed some small-time strong-arm work. In trouble again, this time at the parking lot, Mullidge came to Hugh and Hugh sent him on to Lockridge. Lockridge fixed the charge by spreading some money around. After that, Lockridge felt that Mullidge owed him, and from time to time, Mullidge did small jobs for Lockridge. Mullidge didn't contact Lockridge through his office, but through Alice Jarman. That kept Lockridge clear in case anything went bad.

"The numbers in Mullidge's wallet," Art said.

"I'll make book you'll find Alice Jarman's number there," I said.

"Where's Hugh now?" I asked.

"You're not going to believe me," Coleman said.

But I believed him. At least the whorehouse part of it.

❧ ❧ ❧

We left Ben Coleman in the interrogation room with Lieutenant Bartholome. He had a lot more to tell that we were interested in, but more than anything else, we wanted Hugh Muffin. Coleman could wait. We went down to Art's office and closed the door behind us.

"I'd need a tank division to get in there," Art said. "Or a company of paratroops."

"I've never heard of the place before," I said.

"You, Hump?" Art asked.

"A black I met at a Hawks game said Madame Fiona had girl-pussy out there that you wouldn't believe. That's all I heard."

"A whorehouse? Is that all it is?"

"That's the pleasure part of it," Art said. "About five or six years ago, four rich guys got together and founded the Royal Hart Hunting Club. They had the idea of importing all kinds of African game and putting it into a preserve. Kill your own lion or rhino without going all the way to Africa. They sold shares and memberships, and they began buying up land. They even built a thirty-room hunting lodge. Very plush. Before trouble hit, they'd put together three hundred acres of land and were dickering for another seven hundred. But the roof fell in. All the groups that love animals got on their backs. The newspapers, the TV, the environmental groups, the humane society. A number of court suits were thrown at them."

"I remember it now," I said. "They gave it up, the whole idea."

"Right. And after a time, all that was left was the lodge and about fifty acres of land. It turned into a sort of rich man's drinking club. Two years ago, one of the original founders died and the other three lost interest. The lodge and the land went on the block. A go-between bought it for something in the area of a million dollars. That seems like a lot, but the lodge was worth almost that. The real buyer, it turned out, was the Black Mafia."

"You've got to be kidding," I said.

"That's what the newspapers call them. We call them the Black Eight. Slim Ed Brownlee of Savannah, Jimmy Freestone of Macon, Bubba White of Augusta, Warden Pike of Atlanta…"

"This Warden Pike of Atlanta, you got a picture of him?"

"An old one." Art brought a file from a cabinet in the corner of the room and opened it on his desk. "Pike keeps a low profile now. A *Journal* photographer tried to take his picture a couple of years ago and got a broken camera and a broken arm." He dug out an arrest photo and passed it to me. "Here he is."

The photo went back perhaps ten years, but it was unmistakably The Man. Hump looked at it over my shoulder and nodded at me. I returned it to Art. He dropped it back in the file. "That was Pike's only arrest. He was pimping then, and got in a row with a rival pimp. Why the interest?"

"Just curious."

"You sure?"

I thought I'd better change the subject. "You got a layout on the club?"

"Yeah." He returned Pike's folder to the cabinet and dug around for another. "When Intelligence got the word that the Black Eight bought the lodge, we ran down two of the founders and a number of people who worked there. This is the picture we got. We added to that some info we got from a construction crew that made improvements after the place changed hands."

Art brought out a rolled-up paper and spread it on his desk. The three of us leaned over it.

"It looks easier than it really is," Art said. "When the Black Eight took over the place, they decided to use only the area around the lodge. They fenced it off, two fences ten feet high. You might get past the outer one. The inside one has an electric charge, enough to stun a bull. One gate, and that's the only way in or out. Two headhunters at the gate at all times, well armed. At least one more gun up here at the lodge, on the porch if the weather's not too bad. A jeep that patrols the inside of the fence, but no way of knowing how regular the rounds are. A driver and a shotgun rider. Besides that, there's probably some kind of alarm system, but we're not sure where it is or what it is."

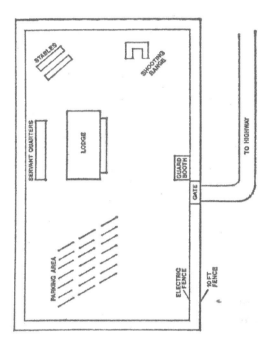

"So much for going over the fence," Hump said. "How do you get through the gate?"

"All you need is your name on a list that's kept at the gate."

I grinned at Art. "You could storm the place."

"On Coleman's say-so? To start a war ... and that's what it'd be ... I need more than that. Right now, all I want to do is talk with Hugh Muffin." He rolled up the map and slipped a rubber band around it. "No, my best bet is to stake the place out and wait until Hugh comes out. Of course, if he finds out we've got Coleman, he might never come out." He tossed the drawing into the cabinet drawer and slammed it shut. "That's some client you've got there, Jim."

"Not my client, and you know it"

"Who is?" Art asked.

I pushed that aside, "You're going to have to trust me one last time, Art. I can't tell you how I know or why I know. Hump'll back me in this. By morning the word'll be out that you want Muffin. I don't care how quiet you try to keep it, they'll know. And as soon as they know, Hugh'll be dead and gone. You won't even find a tooth of a shirt button. Vanished. Right, Hump?"

"He'll be dead within minutes." Hump nodded. "Believe him, Art."

"I'm not that dumb," Art said. "It's a matter of racket ties they wouldn't want him to talk about. If he's not tied in, then what the hell's he doing out there?"

I let him believe that. It was easier than explaining that I was working for Warden Pike, The Man, and that Pike would have Hugh's hide because of his part in the death of Emily Campbell. It would take all night and part of the day to explain all that.

"Shit," I said to Hump, "you can't put anything over on Art."

"Right," Hump said.

"I think I've got a solution. Hump and I might be able to get him out of there."

"Don't volunteer me, white man," Hump said.

"Part of twenty thousand dollars, for an hour's work?"

"Half? I'm with you."

"It'll be rough, and that's if we get through the gate in the first place." I stepped away from the desk. "We need one more man, a black who's good with a gun."

Hump shrugged. "I don't know anybody that dumb. It's not just the time in there. It's all that running for years afterwards."

"I might know one," Art said. "Jim Winters. He's a cop."

"Him along, if it backfires, it could make trouble for the department."

"If he'll do it, he goes on leave as of yesterday."

"Try him," I said.

"A bit too squeaky-clean looking," Hump said.

I looked Jim Winters over. He was an inch or so over six feet, broad-shouldered and flat-waisted. His hair was short and his sideburns looked regulation. He seemed cool and tough. Maybe it was the cop uniform that threw us. Still, I could see what Hump meant.

"How do you dress?"

"Super cool." He was talking to Hump, not to me. "The big man here knows what I mean."

"Got you." Hump put a hand on Winters' shoulder. "Get into your street clothes."

As soon as Winters left, I told Art I needed to make a private call. Art left reluctantly, pulling the door closed behind him. I explained the con to Hump while I looked up Wenzel Brown's home number in the phone book. Hump said it sounded like fun, and too bad it wasn't for real. I got an outside line and dialed. A man with the deep, chesty tones of a preacher answered.

"This is Hardman. I was told I could call you."

"Yes, Mr. Hardman, what can I do for you?"

"A small favor," I said.

"Small or large," Wenzel Brown said, "our mutual friend said I was to give you all the help you needed."

"This is more on the order of pleasure."

"Perhaps you'd better explain it," Brown said.

"You know Hump Evans?"

"The football player?" He laughed. "I've heard legendary stories about Mr. Evans."

"Hump is working with me on that job for our mutual friend. But tonight he's off. and he asked me for a favor." I motioned to Hump. "Here he is now. I'll let him explain what he wants."

Hump took the phone. "Mr. Brown? Hump Evans here. I know this may be an odd request. But I've been hearing a lot about Madame Fiona's for the last year or so. I wonder if you could fix it so that I could make a visit." Hump listened. "Me and a friend from out of town. Roy White. He does some gambling up around Detroit." Hump looked at me and winked. "No, not Hardman. It's past his bedtime. And me, you know I wouldn't want to bother those sweetmeat girls." He stopped and listened. He laughed. "Rumors, Mr. Brown, just rumors. I don't know why those particular girls would tell lies like that about me." Hump nodded at me. "Will you be there tonight? That's too bad. Some other time, then. And they'll have my name at the gate? Thank you, Mr. Brown."

I took the phone. "Hardman again. That business for our friend. The next time you're in touch with him, you can tell him it'll be finished in the next day or two."

"I will, Mr. Hardman. Good night."

On the drive out of town, I talked through the drill with Hump and Jim Winters. It seemed simple enough, almost too simple. "I saw it in a movie once that starred Alan Ladd," I said.

Hump grinned at me. "Before my time, old man."

"How does it sound to you, Winters?"

He shrugged. "It's as good as any on short notice. If it doesn't work, we won't have but about thirty seconds to worry about it."

"That long, you sure?" Hump said, mock-seriously.

"Well," Winters said, grinning past me, "give or take a second or two."

Ahead of us, I could see the braking lights on Art's unmarked police car. I slowed and followed him when he pulled off the highway. We were on a horseshoe turnoff beside a rest stop and picnic area that the state kept up. As soon as we were off the highway, Jim Winters shifted in his seat and looked through the rear window. "I think somebody's following us. You expecting anybody else?"

"No." I braked and we waited. A few seconds later, an old clunker went by. It looked like a '53 Chevy. The headlights could stand adjusting, and it needed a muffler. I wondered how much of a payoff it took to get that one an inspection sticker, if it had one. The Chevy went by without slowing, and Winters laughed and said, "Must not be."

I pulled in deeper and parked behind Art. To our left, was the dark green building that housed the toilets. To our right, encircled by the road, the horseshoe area dotted with leaf-covered picnic tables. We got out of the car and walked over to meet Art and the two uniformed cops with him. They were shivering and moving around, trying to keep warm. Art looked grim and unhappy, like he didn't like the whole idea very much. "We'll wait here. If you get in and out without trouble, head for us. If we hear gunfire, we'll try to get to the gate, or we'll barricade the road out and wait for you. I'm not sure what good that'll do you. Maybe none."

I patted Art on the shoulder and we left him. I opened the trunk of my car and handed Hump the keys. The trunk looked like a weapons locker. Art had outfitted us from the mass of confiscated guns in one of the storerooms. I'd picked a sawed-off shotgun with a cut-down stock and a handful of shells. Winters chose an Ml carbine and two spare clips. Hump said he'd stay with his handgun. Art warned us that there might be a frisk at the gate. On that chance, both Hump and Winters selected pistols to be found carrying when they reached the gate. Their personal guns, the ones they'd use inside the compound, were in the trunk.

"One last question, Hump?" I pushed the shotgun and the Ml carbine to the forward part of the trunk.

"Yeah?"

"Why'd you change Jim's name?"

"Roy White's a real guy. Did some book for me a time or two. If this comes off, it might be better if nobody knows Jim's real name."

"How about this Roy White?" Jim asked.

"They go looking for Roy, they'll find a tombstone in Cleveland."

"Luck," I said. I got in and nodded at Hump.

Hump slammed the trunk door closed and I was in the cramped, closed darkness, smelling the exhaust fumes and gun oil. Of all the goddamn silly places to be.

CHAPTER SEVENTEEN

It was smooth enough, at first. I guess that was while we were still on the highway. When we turned onto the club's access road, it was another thing altogether. Bumps and ruts and potholes, so that I had to put a hand on the trunk door and press myself down. I used the arm like a spring, relaxing it so that I rode with the jumps and lurches. The fumes were still bad and my head hurt. For a time, I thought I might throw up my scotch and cognac and single slice of roast beef. I might have, except that I felt the car slowing and easing to a stop, and there were other things to worry about.

I heard voices, muffled through the steel and glass and upholstery. I knew it could blow up now, and I found myself holding my breath and letting it hiss out slowly, careful that there wasn't a whistle. The maddening part was that I couldn't understand what they were saying. I couldn't tell if it was an inquisition out there in the cold wind, or sports talk about the point spread in the conference playoffs a couple of days ahead. And to cap it all off, I began to get a cramp in my right leg. It was in the calf and, as it knotted, it felt like polio must feel. I scraped the back of my hand moving it down the length of my body to rub the knot of old muscle. Maybe that was just tension, because it began to relax when I heard a booming laugh that must have been Hump's. Two or three others joined him, and I knew that we were past the first hurdle.

Seconds later, the car doors slammed and we were off and moving again. The road we were on now was flat and level, probably paved, and the fact that my weight wasn't shifting from foot to head meant it was going in a fairly straight line. The parking lot must be ahead and to the left of the lodge. About the time I'd decided that we were never going to make it, I felt Hump slowing and easing to a stop. I reached around behind me and got Hump's .38 and Winters' .357. I placed those near my knees and reached up to grip a metal ridge on the trunk door above me. The car doors opened and closed and, a few seconds later, there was a tap on the trunk door.

"Ready, Hardman?"

I tapped back at him. The key scraped in the lock and the lock clicked. I held the door so it wouldn't swing up, instead letting it open only four or five inches. I passed the guns out to Hump.

"Fans of mine back there," Hump said. "How you feeling?"

"Half dead."

"One stud on the porch. Count off a slow three minutes and then come running."

"Right."

"From now."

I started the count. To be safe, I put out a hand and covered the lock catch. Better a banged-up hand than getting locked in again. The cool air blew in on me and I felt my head clearing. The calf of my right leg still felt numb. I hoped that would go away as soon as I put some weight on it I reached one hundred and eighty and gave it another twenty, just to be sure that the confinement wasn't making me count fast

At two hundred, I let the trunk door swing upward and scrambled over the side. The right leg caught again. I didn't have time to argue with it, so I reached down and hit it a good lick with my fist. That wouldn't cure it, but it might stun it. In one hand, I took the M1 carbine with two spare clips taped to the stock. In the other, my sawed-off shotgun with the cut-down stock. Crossing the parking lot, I stayed low, in among the cars as far as they went, and sprinted the last fifty or so yards across in the open to the porch. Jim Winters stepped from behind a column and waved at me.

"Where's Hump?"

"Off in the bushes."

I handed Winters the M1 carbine. He stripped the tape from the spare clips and put the clips in his pocket. He drew the bolt back and threw it forward, putting a round in the carbine's chamber.

"Ready," he said.

A few seconds later, Hump parted the hedge at the end of the porch and stepped up to our level. He tossed the thick roll of two-inch adhesive tape to me. "Better than rope, any day."

"The same Alan Ladd movie," I said.

I moved to the left of the door and Winters went to the right. Hump faced the door squarely and raised his hand to knock. At the last second he turned and grinned at me. "My fan out there at the gate said to ask for Curly, says she's pure black tiger."

"Ask for her, then."

"Just wanted your permission." Hump hit the door panel a couple of hard licks. On a count of about twenty, the door opened. A little black man in a white jacket stood there, squinting at us. "Yes, sir. Are you expected?"

"I'm Hump Evans and this is my friend, Roy White." Hump pointed to his right, toward the darkness where Winters was.

The little man leaned his head through the door frame and turned to look. Winters leaned in and put the barrel of the carbine on the tip of the little man's nose.

"Ask us in nice," Hump said. "Real nice."

The little man blinked. "Yes, sir, you're expected. Come right in."

Hump went in first, the pistol up and at the ready. I wasn't far behind, with the shotgun against the side of my hip. Winters stepped in to the right of Hump, swinging the carbine to cover that area of the room.

"Sit still," I said.

You had to say this for the Black Eight: they'd kept the millionaire playpen up to scratch. The parquet floor shone from the waxing and buffing. The dark drapes that covered the windows were clean and crisp. A large crystal chandelier, high above the lobby, sparkled and gleamed, dust-free.

To the right, under the sweep of Winters' carbine, was the bar. It was done in rattan, with drawings of African animals covering the walls. Behind the bar, above the collection of bottles, there was a large mural of the bush landscape. There was no one behind the bar, so I assumed that the little black man doubled as bartender and doorman.

I tossed the roll of tape to Hump. "The doorman."

I kept my shotgun on the group straight ahead. Four black men and two black women. They were in a kind of living room set, a long, oversized sofa and two soft chairs angled in to face each other across a low round coffee table made of some kind of dark wood. Behind them there was a sort of *Citizen Kane* fireplace with two or three five-foot logs burning in it.

"It looks like a slow night," Jim Winters said.

"Fine with me." I moved in the direction of the group near the fireplace. "You two on the sofa … on your feet. Over to the sofa."

Two hard and mean-looking young men got up slowly and edged over to the sofa. One of them, his face contoured with the craters and ridges of an old case of bad skin, said, "This'll get you dead."

"Not tonight."

To the left, dark now, a dining room. I motioned in that direction, and Jim Winters circled behind me and went in and beyond. Hump finished with the little black man and came over to me. "The men first. Hands behind their backs, mouths taped."

Hump began with the hard-ass with the scarred face. I moved around until I was at the end of the sofa, the shotgun pointing down the line of heads. The message was there, and the men sat rigid and quiet while Hump worked his way down the length of the sofa. As he was finishing up the last man, Winters came back. "Kitchen's dark. Nobody there."

"Watch the front window."

Winters moved over and pushed the drapes aside. "Nothing, so far."

"Keep watching." I walked over and faced the two women across the coffee table. "On the women, just the hands, to start with." I dipped the shotgun so that it pointed toward the floor. "Where's Hugh Muffin?"

"I don't know any Hugh Muffin," the older woman said. She was around forty, big and fleshy. Probably Madame Fiona. A little too old and wasted to make the cut in the whore racket. And she was tough enough not to be afraid of us. "White man, this is going to make your life miserable."

I nodded at Hump and he tore off a piece of tape about six inches long. He reached around Madame Fiona and slapped it across her mouth. That left only the young girl. Dark skin with the face of an African carving. I waited until Hump had the young girl's hands taped behind her. "Talk to the nice girl."

Hump winked and came around the sofa. He sat on the coffee table, knees against hers, and smiled. "You're not by any chance Curly, are you?"

The girl, wide-eyed and scared, shook her head. "I'm Josie."

"That's too bad. I was told to ask for Curly. If I was here for that reason, I think I'd pick you, Josie. Couldn't help myself."

"Curly's busy upstairs."

"That don't trouble me much." Hump put out a hand and cupped the girl's face. "Josie, we're not here to hurt anybody. Nobody gets hurt. All we want is that white man, that old boar-coon. You know who I mean?"

The girl nodded. "Mr. Hugh."

"Which room's he in?"

Madame Fiona didn't like the way the conversation was going. She lifted the leg closest to Josie and kicked at her. Hump blocked and caught the foot. He held the foot in his hand until I expected to hear bones breaking. When he released it and pushed it aside, it dropped like it was numb.

"Room two, at the head of the stairs and to the right," Josie said. "Curly's with him."

"All right now, I'm going to have to tape your mouth. It won't hurt you." Hump tore off a length of tape. "Breathe through your nose and don't panic." Carefully, gently, like he was dressing a wound, Hump applied the tape to her mouth. Hump stood up and turned to me. "I'd like to come along, like to meet that Curly girl."

"One look," I said, "and then you have to come back and cover the stairs."

"One look."

"We don't know how many rooms are being used. That's where the trouble could come from." I started for the stairs at the right rear of the lobby. "Roy, watch the sofa until Hump comes back."

Winters lined up the carbine on the sofa. "Take two looks. One for me. They're not going anywhere."

At the top of the landing, the stairway led into a hall. The hall branched: one fork leading straight ahead, and two others going sharply left and right. I could hear a radio far away, sifting through the walls, with the bass more complete than anything else. Other than that, it seemed closed for the night. Tucked in until the morning screwing. I only hoped that nobody decided he needed some ice or mixer. That could cut the string and let the pig out.

We passed up Room One and stopped in front of Room two. I tried the door and found it locked. I leaned close to Hump. "Just enough weight to spring the lock. As little noise as you can."

Hump stepped forward and gripped the door knob. He leaned his shoulder against the door. The muscles popped up in his neck. The wood around the lock splintered with no more noise than a cork coming out of a bottle.

I stepped past him and leveled the shotgun. There was a low-wattage bulb burning in the lamp on the nightstand. In that dim light, I saw the girl next to Hugh Muffin pull the sheet over her head. At the same time, Hugh rolled over the edge of the bed and made a run for the chair, where his clothes were piled. We caught him in between, bare-assed and meat slapping on his leg. "Hold it, Uncle Hugh."

Hugh stopped so fast he almost pitched forward. He turned and had the gall to smile. "Oh, it's you. Good to see you."

I waved the shotgun at him. "Back to the bed, Hugh."

As soon as he was seated on the edge of the bed, I circled him to the pile of clothes. I reached under the pile and brought up a pistol. I stuck it in my belt. "How'd you get this through the gate?"

"They don't search me. They know I'm the peaceful type."

Hump was on the other side of the bed. He leaned over and grabbed a handful of sheet. He ripped it away from the girl. "Well, look at what I found."

She was a pretty little thing, the shade of black that looks like it might pass for a long summer's tan. Breasts like hard apples. Instead of being frightened or shy, she grinned up at Hump and opened her legs. "You found me."

"I guess you're Curly."

"You've heard of me?"

"The word's all the way downtown about you."

I hated to break it up, but the time was getting low. We didn't have all night. "Had your two looks?"

"Just about," Hump said. "You mind if I take her downstairs with me?"

"If it's all right with Hugh."

When Hugh said nothing, I nodded at Hump and he scooped her out of the bed with one arm. Curly *wheeeed* a little, but she didn't seem to mind. As they went out the door, I saw an arm come up and wrap around Hump's neck. I followed them to the door and closed it. "You can get dressed now."

Hugh didn't move, at first. "Hardman, is there any special reason you went to all this trouble?"

"I like you, and I didn't want you to get killed," I said.

"I'm not in any danger."

"The shit you say." I wagged the shotgun at the pile of clothes. "Get dressed."

He stood up, and I walked over to the chair and tossed his underwear to him. "Getting through that gate's one thing. Getting back out is a horse of another color."

"You better hope we do."

"You're talking in riddles," Hugh said. He stepped into his shorts and pulled the t-shirt over his head.

"When The Man knows what I know you're just two hundred pounds of bloody meat."

"What's that supposed to mean?"

"The Man'll crook his finger, and you're dead. That'll happen as soon as he knows how responsible you are for the death of Emily Campbell, the little black guy, Ferd, and for sending those two guns after him."

Hugh got into his shirt. "He won't believe that. He knows me better than that."

"He'll believe me when I spread it out for him." I tossed his trousers to him. "I think you guessed he was my client, didn't you?"

He gave me a sour grin. "From the start. It wasn't Arch, and it wasn't me. It had to be him."

"I had a feeling about you," I said. "My guess is that she saw you over at The Man's place. Perhaps she was leaving, in a car driven by Ferd. You were arriving. Or it might have been the other way around. You leaving, Emily arriving."

"It's your story." He zipped his trousers and notched his belt.

"Right after that, something happened to make Emily believe that she was in danger. It must have been a frightening time for her. She couldn't go to The Man. He seemed to be doing business with you, and she must have felt that he'd choose his business over his girlfriend. And you were her father's best friend. She couldn't go to him. He'd probably send her to a psychiatrist." I threw him one shoe and sock. "What scared her, Hugh?"

"What I heard somewhere was that a car barely missed her in a dark parking lot. A near miss, the way I heard it."

"My next guess. She called you or you called her. A meeting was set up. She wanted to convince you that she didn't care what kind of rackets you were in." I tossed him the other sock and shoe. "A meeting was set up for that Monday night. You made yourself an alibi and sent Mullidge to meet her. That was a point-less murder. Emily probably didn't care how many shady deals you made."

Hugh stood up. "Whoever it was didn't like the idea of one person knowing who didn't have to know. The first thing you know, she tells the wrong person."

"And Ferd? He must have figured it out and tried to shake you down."

Hugh got into his jacket, balled up his tie, and shoved it into one pocket. "Him? He never had a bright thought in his life. But you were nosing around, and this man … whoever he was … thought you might prod him into making a connection. The man who killed Ferd met him on the street after his last drop, said he had to see The Man with some important news, and asked for a ride over to the apartment. On the way, he played with a slapjack that Ferd seemed proud of, for some reason. He waited until Ferd parked, looked around to make sure the area was empty, and then hit Ferd on the head a few times. Then he got out and walked over to Whitehall and caught a bus."

"In broad daylight?"

"Why not. People are more trusting in the daytime."

I checked the topcoat and threw it to him. "Why was Mullidge after me?"

"You were fine as long as you believed that Eddie Spence had done all the killing. When you changed your mind, you were in the way."

I decided not to say anything about Lockridge and his girl. It was probably better if Hugh didn't know the police were holding Coleman. "And the try on The Man?"

"Two things. He seemed to be taking Emily's death too seriously. Hiring you, for example. Secondly, he has a rich territory. This man we're talking about and a couple of black friends wanted it—the whole thing: gambling, drugs and women." Hugh laughed at me. "Especially the women."

"Outside and down the stairs."

I edged the door open with my shoe and wagged the shotgun at him. I followed him down the hall and down the stairs, and into the lobby of the lodge. Hump met us at the bottom of the stairs, leaning on the banister, with the .38 pointed upward. When I passed him he grinned and said, "Took so long, I was about to come looking for you."

"Hugh likes to talk while he's dressing."

Hugh stopped and looked around. His eyes shifted past the six who were taped up on the sofa and paused on Curly, who was in one of the easy chairs beside the coffee table. Hump had found her a man's raincoat, which she wore carelessly wrapped across her. Hugh smiled at her. "Considering the way I was interrupted, I think you can understand why there won't be any payment tonight."

"Hugh, that's all right," Curly said. "Call it a Christmas present."

Jim Winters stepped away from the window and dropped the drapes back in place. "Had one visitor. Hump tapped him out."

"I hardly touched him." Hump moved around the sofa and stared down at Curly. "Man, oh man," he said almost under his breath.

I followed the point of Winters' carbine, and saw the pudgy black man stretched out beside the bar. The tape on his hands and mouth seemed unnecessary. He was out.

"We ready?"

Hump and Winters said they were.

"Tape and muzzle the girl," I said.

"Aw." Hump put on an act. He looked downcast. "I was thinking about taking Curly along for me."

"It might get wasted out there."

"I wouldn't want that to happen. Not to this girl." He finished her hands and duck-walked around the chair to face her. "Some other time then, Curly." He kissed her and then fitted the strip of tape over her mouth. "And you better believe it."

"Still clear outside," Jim Winters said from the window.

"Now Hugh. Tape his mouth good. Hands in front of him, so he'll be comfortable."

While Hump worked over Hugh, I went to the sofa. "We're leaving now. Nobody's hurt, and nobody's going to be hurt. Just stay where you are. Anybody comes out of that front door in the next ten minutes is going to get a load of shot thrown at them."

The hard eyes above the tape just stared at me. Only the young girl, Josie, nodded that she understood.

We crossed the porch and the parking lot without any trouble. Hump unlocked the trunk, and we boosted Hugh in and closed the door over him. So far, it was going well. I didn't even like to think how well it was going. That might ruin it, just thinking.

I got in the back seat, down on my knees on the floorboards. The shotgun was on the seat where I could reach it. The muzzle was pointed to the left, in the direction of the guard booth. Hump and Winters were in the front. Hump started it up, backed around in a half circle, and pointed toward the gate. If it went well, Hump was supposed to ease down and glide through the gate without stopping while he made some bawdy remark about Curly.

We were twenty yards out of the parking lot when it went bad. An alarm bell or a fire bell went off. It didn't matter which it was. From the volume and the clarity, it sounded like it was probably mounted on the front of the lodge. So someone back at the lodge had touched it off. Now the gate was alerted. There was no way we could get through without a fight. We could only hope that the patrol jeep was in one of the far areas and wouldn't be able to beat us to the gate.

I reached over the seat and slapped Hump on the shoulder. "Floor it." I turned and leaned closer to Winters. "When we get close, put a few rounds into the gate house."

"So much for hurried planning," Hump said.

I rolled down the window on the side of the car facing the gate booth. I put the shotgun on the window ledge and waited.

Now they had the pig in the chute and, without some luck, it'd get screwed and barbecued.

CHAPTER EIGHTEEN

"Headlights out, Hump," Winters yelled, and we began the run for the gate. Ahead of us, as I looked between Hump and Winters, I could see one of the gate guards run out of the booth. He grabbed the gate-half nearest the guard booth and began to fumble with the latch that held it back in place. The range was impossible for my shotgun. Even knowing that, I thought I ought to worry him some. "Watch your head, Hump." I poked the shotgun out the window and pointed it in the guard's general direction. I let one barrel go. It wasn't the best position for firing a shotgun, and it almost kicked out of my hands.

"Shit," Hump shouted back at me, "I think you got my eyebrows."

I steadied the shotgun again and let the other barrel go in the direction of the guard booth. While I pulled the shotgun back into the car and broke it open, Winters leaned out of the passenger window with his Ml carbine. He ripped off part of a magazine, spraying the gate opening. It was like hanging a big sign out there: don't go near it. I thumbed out the spent shells and reloaded.

Fifty or seventy-five yards from the gate, I thought we had made it. We were almost there, and it seemed that they hadn't fired at us at all. I began to feel that the fire we'd poured in their direction had made them dig holes, holes they weren't about to climb out of until we were out of the compound and gone.

The jeep headlights hit us then, quartering in from the passenger side of the car.

"Shit!" Jim Winters turned his body and braced the carbine on the window ledge. He emptied the rest of the first magazine in a single burst. The barrel of the carbine hit the roof of the car as he moved it upward and ejected the empty clip and jammed another into place. I slid across the seat and got the window down on that side. The jeep lights bounced across me, and then were gone. I knew they were getting close, too close, and I guessed that they would turn soon and move parallel with us, giving the stud with the shotgun his crack at us from deadly range. I put that out of my mind, aimed for the hood of the jeep, and then moved it lower, toward the tires. I let go with both barrels. One headlight went out and the jeep swerved and skidded. In the seat in front of me, Jim Winters opened up with another burst from the carbine. The other headlight crunched and went out.

We flashed by the gate booth and onto the bumpy, rutted road that led to the highway.

"That last part was out of some fucking James Cagney movie," Hump said.

"Only we didn't get hit a single time. That must be some record."

"You crazy?" Winters asked. "The front of this car, I bet you could drain spaghetti through it." Winters leaned back in his seat and dug a hand into his left shoulder. While I watched, blood flowed through his fingers and down his arm. "I've got the proof of it, right here." I dug out a clean handkerchief and handed it to him. He opened the shirt and pressed the folded handkerchief over the wound.

"It's not bad," Winters said, "but it's messing up my good threads."

"The replacement's are on Hump and me," I said.

"Done," Winters said.

Art waited for us at the base of the road, where it joined the main highway. His unmarked police car was wedged across its two-car width. Hump braked and I got out running. Art came around the rear of the car and met me. "Got Hugh. He's in the trunk."

Hump got out and opened the trunk and pulled a dazed Hugh Muffin from the compartment. One of Art's men got Hugh by the elbow and hurried him over to Art's car. "Winters got hit in the shoulder."

"In my car," Art said. "We go by the emergency ward on the way in. We can use the siren, too, if we have to."

I nodded. I was still looking down the road, waiting to see if there was any pursuit. So far, none. Maybe there wasn't going to be any. At least I hoped not, now that we were at the highway. I left Art for the moment, and Hump and I helped Winters into the front seat of the police car.

"Thanks," I said. "And we'll be by to see you tomorrow."

"And don't forget your threads," Hump said.

"I won't." Winters was tired, and it was hurting now that the shock was over. That was the way it was, first like a brick hitting you, then the real pain, after the stunned feeling left you.

I went back to my car and sat in the front seat, next to Hump. We waited while Art jockeyed the car around and headed it back toward Atlanta. For the first mile or so, we stayed with the police car. Then Art put on the siren and left us like we were standing still. It didn't seem to matter, boing left. It was over, and I was getting the shakes. It took me à lot of fumbling around to get the glove compartment open. There was around two swallows of cognac left in the flask. I almost broke a front tooth trying to fit the flask to my mouth. I had my swallow and passed it on to Hump.

"God, I'm shaky," I said.

"Two of us." Hump tilted back his head and finished it off. As he lowered his head, he looked into the rear-view mirror. He passed the empty to me. "Company, Jim. I think it's that clunker again."

"The same one?" I twisted around and tried to get a good look at it. There was a car behind us. It might have been the same one. The headlights were out of line, one pointing skyward and the other toward the road. Beyond that, I couldn't get a good idea of the make or the year.

"Hard to tell," Hump said. "More likely, it's some kid on the way back from seeing his girl out in the country."

"You've always got such reasonable explanations," I said.

"Youth being the way it is today," Hump said, "he had time for one fast fuck and a good-night kiss."

"If it's the same clunker."

I could feel myself relaxing, the pleasant warmth of the cognac spreading from my stomach outward. I tilted the empty flask and got another drop or two. It wasn't enough.

The rest of the way into town, I kept an eye on the car behind us. When we reached the city limits, I told Hump to pull into an empty lot next to a filling station. Hump got into position and we watched the old Chevy go past. I didn't get a look at the driver because the windows seemed fogged over. But the driver didn't seem to be paying any attention to us. He went on by. We gave him a minute or two and started after him. There didn't seem to be any sign of him on the street ahead, so I decided that settled it. I put it out of my mind altogether. All I wanted now was another drink.

We reached the department parking lot a few seconds after Art did. As we turned in, I could see that his doors were open and he was getting out, while a cop in the back seat with Hugh Muffin had him by an elbow and was yanking him out. I motioned Hump to a space about eight or ten cars from Art's, and Hump wheeled into place. I got out and breathed the. cold night air. It stung my lungs and shook me awake.

I could hear Hugh then. They'd taken the tape from his mouth. "It was kidnapping, out and out kidnapping, taking me from the home of a friend at gunpoint …"

"From a whorehouse," Art said.

"From a nightclub," Hugh insisted.

"A black whorehouse," Art said.

It went on and on. Hump came around the side of the car and slapped me on the back. We stood at the rear of the car and waited as they came toward us. Art had Hugh by one elbow, and the other cop was on the other side of him. I didn't see the third cop. I guessed they'd left him at the hospital with Jim Winters. I turned to Hump, about to say that we'd have to drop by the hospital the next day, when a man stepped out from the shadowy line of parked cars. He was between us, facing the approaching line of Art, Hugh and the other cop, and with his back to Hump and me. From the blue raincoat and the size of his body, I knew it was Eddie Spence. Hugh Muffin saw him first and raised his taped hands, as if to protect himself or begin a plea. It didn't get very far. The flat crack of the pistol tore it off. The slugs hit Hugh and threw him back, like he'd been struck by a high-speed car head-on. Even as he was going down, another shot hit him in the back.

It stunned Art at first, the suddenness of it, and then his hand brushed his coat aside and moved for the gun on his hip. Eddie Spence turned slightly and lined up the .45 on him. Art brought his hands up and away from his body. The other cop did the same.

Either Eddie hadn't seen me, or he didn't care. I got the .38 out of my belt and gave Hump a shove that got him out of the line of fire, between two cars. I got into my target-range stance and lined up on the broadest part of Eddie, the body half from the waist up to the bullish neck.

"Eddie!" I yelled at him, "drop it in the road, and put your hands on your head.".

Eddie went still, rigid, but the gun was still pointing at Art. "Is that you, Hardman?"

"Yes. Give it up, Eddie. It's over."

With his back still to me, Eddie said, "I knew you'd find him, Hardman."

"Put it on the ground."

His shoulders jerked in a slight movement, and I knew that he'd made up his mind. He was going to whirl toward me. "I'm not going to jail."

"Eddie, you turn and I'll drop you, so help me. Don't make me do it."

"Do it then." He began his turn. Behind him, as soon as the eye of the .45 left them, Art and the other cop took flying dives to the asphalt. Not wanting to fire, watching Eddie, I almost waited too long. First he was in profile and then in three-quarters and, as he moved to full body again, I still didn't want to fire. The .45 was clear now, up and moving downward as he sighted on me.

"Burn him," Hump hissed at me, "burn him, goddamit!"

I dropped the hammer on him twice, and both slugs hit' him chest high. He spun away, staggering, and fell across the tail end of a car. He slumped there for a few seconds and then he slid off it, loose and lifeless.

Art ran over to him and kicked the .45 away from him. It clattered toward me.

Hump came out of the darkness. "Well, there goes twenty thou and a wasted youth, all in the same night."

"The poor sonofabitch. I guess he was in that clunker, after all. Saw enough to make his guess, and beat us here when I got foxy."

Hump put a hand on my shoulder. "Screw that young love and what it gets you."

That covered Eddie Spence. It belonged on his tombstone. I looked beyond Eddie's body to the pudgy lump that had been Hugh Muffin. The other cop had checked him and now came toward us, shaking his head. "And all the money-grabbing shit, too," I said.

I felt godawful. My head hurt, and I was sick to my stomach. I felt like somebody had crapped on me, and then turned off the water so I couldn't take a shower. Sometimes it was like that.

In the next hour or so, Ben Coleman filled in the blanks on the parts we didn't know. Hugh Muffin had been taking for years, since his first term in the state senate. The longer he remained there, the more clout he had, and the money got better and better. He was on his way to writing the last zero on his first million. And then Emily Campbell looked the wrong way that night in The Man's parking lot and saw him. That had turned it all around. The deaths of Emily and Ferd had been to protect himself, to keep his identity covered. That was as far as he'd planned. And then Eddie Spence had appeared, and he'd seen the other possibility. He could take over The Man's whole Atlanta operation and put in two hand-picked blacks to run it for him. He knew that all the deaths around Emily Campbell would be tied to Eddie Spence, sooner or later. Even the death of The Man. Knowing me, Hugh knew that I'd have to reveal the relationship between The Man and Emily after The Man was dead. That revelation would point it all back to Spence. And Hugh'd be covered, in the closet and clean.

But I started sniffing around in other directions. I even had doubts, as I'd told Coleman, that Eddie had killed Emily. From that time on, I was in the way, a spoiler. That was when Hugh turned Mullidge loose on me and imported the two guns from the Midwest.

With Hugh Muffin dead, Coleman tried to turn back into a Sunday-school teacher. He denied the statement he'd made earlier. Now, he insisted, his only involvement had been as a witness to the deaths of Lockridge and Alice Jarman. Beyond that, he hardly knew Hugh, except as Arch Campbell's friend. In the earlier statement, given while we were planning the raid on the lodge, Coleman had said he'd been investing some of Hugh's dirty money in land and beach-front property, mixing it in and disguising it among the investments he made for Campbell and a few of his friends.

I left Art to deal with all that, to decide how they'd charge Coleman. It was the department's headache, and they were welcome to it.

Hump must have decided that I looked like hell. He said he'd stay the night at my place, just for the company. He drove us through the main part of Peachtree, past all the Christmas decorations, all the light and glitter. The streets were empty and bare and cold, and the decorations seemed pathetic rather than gay. It was Christmas Eve morning, and I still hadn't done any of my shopping. And Marcy would be waiting for me that night, as soon as I'd put some of my scattered parts back together. If I could.

We never did get all of the twenty thousand dollars reward. Most of it had been pledges, anyway, and a lot of it dried up and blew away. Arch Campbell tried his best, and his collection came to around seven thousand dollars. It was better than nothing, but it wasn't the windfall that Hump had been expecting.

The Man came back to Atlanta after New Years, and he breathed fire for the first hour or so. He didn't like the raid on the lodge, and the others in the Black Eight were just waiting for him to get back to town and vote on whether to start a new landfill with Hump and me. After he calmed down a bit and heard us out, he agreed to cool the steam from the ruckus. We'd given him something else to worry about: the identity of the two hand-picked blacks whom Hugh had planned to put in his place. If he ever found out who they were, I guess he started the landfill with them.

It wasn't a bad Christmas season, if you weren't Emily Campbell or Eddie Spence or Hugh Muffin. Or any of the other dead.

ABOUT THE AUTHOR

Ralph Dennis isn't a household name... but he should be. He is widely considered among crime writers as a master of the genre, denied the recognition he deserved because his twelve *Hardman* books, which are beloved and highly sought-after collectables now, were poorly packaged in the 1970s by Popular Library as a cheap men's action-adventure paperbacks with numbered titles.

Even so, some top critics saw past the cheesy covers and noticed that he was producing work as good as John D. MacDonald, Raymond Chandler, Chester Himes, Dashiell Hammett, and Ross MacDonald.

The *New York Times* praised the *Hardman* novels for "expert writing, plotting, and an unusual degree of sensitivity. Dennis has mastered the genre and supplied top entertainment." The *Philadelphia Daily News* proclaimed *Hardman* "the best series around, but they've got such terrible covers..."

Unfortunately, Popular Library didn't take the hint and continued to present the series like hack work, dooming the novels to a short shelf-life and obscurity... except among generations of crime writers, like novelist Joe R. Lansdale (the *Hap & Leonard* series) and screenwriter Shane Black (the *Lethal Weapon* movies), who've kept Dennis' legacy alive through word-of-mouth and by acknowledging his influence on their stellar work.

Ralph Dennis wrote three other novels that were published outside of the *Hardman* series—*Atlanta, Deadman's Game* and

MacTaggart's War—but he wasn't able to reach the wide audience, or gain the critical acclaim, that he deserved during his lifetime.

He was born in 1931 in Sumter, South Carolina, and received a masters degree from University of North Carolina, where he later taught film and television writing after serving a stint in the Navy. At the time of his death in 1988, he was working at a bookstore in Atlanta and had a file cabinet full of unpublished novels.

Brash Books will be releasing the entire *Hardman* series, his three other published novels, and his long-lost manuscripts.

Made in the USA
San Bernardino,
CA